Incredible
Ivy
of
Iowa

Here's what readers from around the country are saying about Johnathan Rand's *AMERICAN CHILLERS:*

"Now that I finished reading DANGEROUS DOLLS OF DELAWARE, I had to get rid of all my dolls and put them in a box in the basement. That book creeped me out so bad!"

-Erin V., age 12, Virginia

"Your books are so cool! I'm reading OGRES OF OHIO right now. Keep writing!"

-Jaden,age unknown, Illinois

"I love your books! We bought some new American Chillers for vacation and it was so hard to wait until we went on vacation to read them!"

-Mason, age 9, Minnesota

"I am really excited for your new book to come out! Once it is out, I will buy it. I want to buy everything at Chillermania! You write the best books!"

-Caleb C., Age 10, New Mexico

"I used to think that American Chillers would give me nightmares, so I was nervous to read them. My friend gave me INVISIBLE IGUANAS OF ILLINOIS and I loved it! Thanks for writing such great books!"

-Brandon B, age 9, West Virginia

"I just read NUCLEAR JELLYFISH OF NEW JERSEY and it was amazing! What a great book!"

-Devan W., age 12, Wisconsin

"My Dad and I read MUTANT MAMMOTHS OF MONTANA, and we both loved it. He says he wishes that he had your books when he was a kid. How come you didn't write them sooner?"

-Tori Y., age 8, New Mexico

"I loved it when you came to my school! That was so much fun! I never used to like reading before, but I love your books!"

-Carlos G., age 11, Nevada

"I love your books! My mom says that it's your fault that I have bad dreams at night, but I can't stop reading American Chillers. My sister says I have an addiction to your books."

-Emerson R., age 9, California

"My teacher let me borrow MONSTER MOSQUITOES OF MAINE and our new puppy chewed it up. We had to buy a new one at the store. But the best part was my dad bought me my own copy to keep!"

-David B., age 8, Michigan

"Your books totally freak me out. I can't read them before bedtime because then I can't sleep. So, I read them during school and on the bus. You write the best books ever! And please put my name in one of your books."

-Mackenzee F., age 9, Alabama

"Your books rock! My aunt met you two times, I think, and you wrote in my IDAHO ICE BEAST book 'Chill Out, Matt!' I love your glasses, by the way. Keep writing AWESOME books!"

-Matt M., age 11, Wisconsin

"My brother let me borrow NEBRASKA NIGHTCRAWL-ERS, and I thought it was great! I read it twice, and I even did a book report on it!"

-Carly T., Age 9, Nebraska

"Dude, you have to write faster! I've read all of your books, and I can't wait for more. Can you hurry and write more?"

-Connor P., age 10, Connecticut

"I met you at your store, Chillermania, last year, and we bought a ton of your books! Thanks for autographing all of them!"

-Bailey D., age 12, Indiana

"I like your books, but I'm just writing this note because my sister says that you won't print it. She says you have people make up the Chiller Blurbs. Please print this so I can prove her wrong like I always do."

-Gabe K., age 8, Oklahoma

Got something cool to say about Johnathan Rand's books? Let us know, and we might publish it right here! Send your short blurb to:

Chiller Blurbs
281 Cool Blurbs Ave.
Topinabee, MI 49791

Other books by Johnathan Rand:

#40: Incredible Ivy of Iowa

Johnathan Rand

An AudioCraft Publishing, Inc. book

This book is a work of fiction. Names, places, characters and incidents are used fictitiously, or are products of the author's very active imagination.

Book storage and warehouses provided by Chillermania!©
Indian River, Michigan

No part of this published work may be reproduced in whole or in part, by any means, without written permission from the publisher. For information regarding permission, contact: AudioCraft Publishing, Inc., PO Box 281, Topinabee Island, MI 49791

American Chillers #40: Incredible Ivy of Iowa
ISBN 13-digit: 978-1-893699-34-2

Librarians/Media Specialists:
PCIP/MARC records available **free of charge** at
www.americanchillers.com

Cover illustration by Dwayne Harris
Cover layout and design by Sue Harring

Printed in USA

INCREDIBLE
IVY
OF
IOWA

VISIT CHILLERMANIA!

WORLD HEADQUARTERS FOR BOOKS BY JOHNATHAN RAND!

CHILLERMANIA!

**I-75 Exit 313
then south
1 mile!**

Visit the HOME for books by Johnathan Rand! Featuring books, hats, shirts, bookmarks and other cool stuff not available anywhere else in the world! Plus, watch the American Chillers website for news of special events and signings at *CHILLERMANIA!* with author Johnathan Rand! Located in northern lower Michigan, on I-75! Take exit 313 . . . then south 1 mile! For more info, call (231) 238-0338. And be afraid! Be veeeery afraaaaaaiiiid . . . .

1

"There it is," I said to Jarvis, with my finger against the cool glass of the store window. "That's the bike I'm going to get."

Jarvis took one look at the bike and turned to face me. His eyes were wide, and his playful grin said it all: he didn't believe me. He didn't think there was any way I would be able to afford the bike.

"It's a cool looking bike, Kayla," he said, nodding toward the window. "But you told me that your parents aren't going to buy it for you. Where are *you* going to get the money?"

"I'll get a job, and I'll earn it," I replied confidently.

"Kayla," Jarvis said, again nodding toward the bicycle on the other side of the glass. "That bicycle is almost three hundred dollars. Where are *you* going to get a job that pays *that* kind of money? You're eleven years old."

"You wait and see," I said, putting my hands on my hips. "I'll get it."

"You'd be a lot better off saving your money for something like this," Jarvis said, and he pulled out his new, red pocket knife to show me. I knew that he'd wanted it, and he'd been saving his money for nearly a year. It was a Swiss Army knife, and it had not only a blade, but nearly a dozen more useful tools that folded neatly within the handle.

"That's a nice pocket knife," I said, "but it only cost you thirty dollars. My bike costs a lot more."

Jarvis returned the knife to his pocket, and I took another long look at the bicycle. It was candy apple red with big, knobby tires for tearing through trails. The seat and handlebars were black. It was sleek and shiny, and it was the coolest looking bicycle I'd ever seen. It certainly was a lot better than the old bike that I was still riding around, the bike that had been my brother's before he outgrew it.

"Well," Jarvis said. "Good luck. I mean, it's a very cool bicycle and all, but that's a lot of money to earn in one summer."

Yes, Jarvis was right. The exact price of the bike was two hundred ninety-nine dollars, and I still hadn't figured out how I'd get all that money. I thought about babysitting. I thought about lemonade stands and bake sales. I thought about mowing lawns. I thought about anything I could do to earn enough money to buy the bicycle. And although I couldn't really come up with anything right away, I refused to give up. I refused to give up dreaming. I refused to think that I wouldn't be able to earn the money.

I knew I could.

I knew I *would*.

And I was certain, beyond any shadow of a doubt, that I would have enough money to buy the bicycle before the end of the summer.

I just didn't know that it might cost me my life—and Jarvis's life—to get it.

When I got home that afternoon, there was a strange vehicle in the driveway. It was a white pickup truck. On the driver's side door, the words *Incredible Ivy* were printed in black letters. There was a phone number beneath the wording, and the words and telephone number were circled with stalks of leafy vines of red and green ivy. Beneath the vines were the words *Prairie City, Iowa* in blue letters. I hadn't seen the truck before, and I wondered if it belonged to a friend of one of my parents.

I parked my brother's old bicycle in the garage and

went into the house. Dad was standing in the living room, talking to a man I hadn't seen before. He was tall and thin, with short, black hair peppered with gray. Dad and the man looked at me when I came in.

"And here she is right now," my dad said, smiling and gesturing with his arm. "Mr. Nelson, this is my daughter, Kayla."

The man named Mr. Nelson extended his hand, and I extended mine. We shook.

"Hi," I said.

Mr. Nelson's eyes sparkled. "It's very nice to meet you, Miss Blaisdale," he said.

I was a little surprised, and maybe a little embarrassed. No one ever calls me 'Miss Blaisdale.' Everyone calls me by my first name, Kayla.

"Mr. Nelson is an old friend of mine," my dad explained. "He's opening a business not far away, and he's looking for people who are interested in a little part-time work."

"That's right," Mr. Nelson said with a nod. His face became very serious. "Your father tells me you've been looking to earn some money."

"Um, yeah," I said, nodding. "I've been trying to think of things I can do, but nothing is really coming to mind. And I'm too young to have a *real* part-time job."

"Well," Mr. Nelson continued, "you're certainly not

too young to help me out around my farm. That is, of course, if you're interested."

"Yeah, sure," I said, not bothering to even ask what kind of work he wanted me to do. I was so excited at the chance to earn some money that it didn't matter what the job was. At that point, I would've done *anything*.

"There's a lot of work that needs to be done," Mr. Nelson said, "and I might need someone else to help. Do you have a friend who would also like to earn a little extra money?"

Without even thinking, I nodded my head and spoke.

"I'll bet my friend, Jarvis DeMotte, would love to earn some money."

Mr. Nelson frowned, and his look became serious. "Is he a good worker? Your father tells me that you work very hard, and that's good. But how about your friend? Does he work as hard as you?"

Again, I nodded. "Jarvis would be a great worker," I said. "And I know that he would love to earn some extra money."

"Perfect!" Mr. Nelson said, clasping his hands together. "Do you think you and Jarvis could come to my farm tomorrow? I can show you around, and you can start working in the afternoon."

I thought about this for a moment. The next day

was Friday, and I didn't have anything going on. It was June, and school had just let out for the summer . . . so, I didn't have any homework to worry about. And even if I did have something going on, I would change it, especially now that I had a real, paying job!

"That would be great!" I said excitedly. "I'll call Jarvis right now and let him know."

"My farm is only a couple of miles away," Mr. Nelson said. "You and your friend can probably ride your bikes there. I'll draw you a map, but it's very easy to find. And be sure to wear old clothing, because you're going to get dirty."

Mr. Nelson and my dad continued talking, and I excused myself and went to my bedroom. I grabbed my phone and called Jarvis.

"Guess what?" I asked.

"What?" Jarvis replied.

"We have jobs!" I said.

There was a long pause. Then:

"What do you mean?" Jarvis asked.

"Just what I said!" I answered. "There's a guy here named Mr. Nelson. He's a friend of my dad's, and he wants us to work at his farm. We need to be there tomorrow at noon."

Jarvis paused. "You mean a job that pays *money?*"

"Yes!" I answered.

Again, Jarvis paused. "What do we have to do?"

"Who cares?" I said. "It's a job. We're going to earn money."

"How much?" Jarvis asked.

"I don't know that, either," I said. "But it's a *job*, Jarvis! We're going to earn money. I'm going to earn enough for my bicycle, just like I told you!"

Jarvis agreed to meet me at my house at eleven-thirty the next morning. From there, we'd ride our bikes to Mr. Nelson's farm. And while I had no idea what duties the job required, I didn't care. I would do anything. Mr. Nelson had told me to wear old clothes, so I figured most of the work would be outside.

I was so excited that night that I had a hard time falling asleep. I read for a long time, and then I put my book down and turned off the light. I closed my eyes, but it seemed like my eyelids kept opening on their own. I turned on the light again, read some more, and then turned off the light again and put my book on the stand beside my bed.

A job, I thought as I lay awake in bed, my head resting on the pillow. My bedroom window was open, and the soothing sound of crickets drifted through the screen.

A real, honest-to-goodness, paying job. I'm going to get that bicycle, for sure.

I finally fell asleep, dreaming about my new bicycle,

dreaming about speeding over trails, through puddles, and through the woods. All of this, I imagined in my mind . . . .

But I never imagined the terrible things that were about to happen to Jarvis and me at a small farm near Prairie City called *Incredible Ivy*.

"I never knew this place was here," Jarvis said, turning his head from left to right.

We were on our bikes, stopped at a big, green, steel gate. A large sign on it read:

STOP!
PROPERTY OF INCREDIBLE IVY
PRAIRIE CITY, IA
NO TRESPASSING.

The gate was secured by a chain with a padlock.

"My dad said that the place is pretty new," I said. "I

guess some of the buildings have been here for a while, and others were just built."

I had my phone in my back pocket, and I pulled it out to check the time. It was 11:55 AM. We were five minutes early.

As I returned the phone to my pocket, I heard tires crunching gravel in the distance. Jarvis and I turned to see Mr. Nelson's white truck coming toward us. We rolled our bikes to the side of the driveway and waited for his arrival.

We spent the next hour following Mr. Nelson as he gave us a tour of the farm. First of all, he showed us the fields of ivy. Some of the vines were green, some were red, which I thought was strange. He explained that the green plants were male, and the red plants were female.

"I didn't even know there was such a thing as male and female plants," I said.

"It's not uncommon at all," said Mr. Nelson.

Then, he showed us the warehouse that he used for storing equipment and farm machinery. The warehouse was a large, box-shaped building with white, metal siding. Inside, parked on the hard-packed dirt, was a large tractor that was identical to the kind my dad has. It was green and yellow and taller than me. When I was little, Dad used to give me rides around our yard and in the back field. When I got bigger, he showed me how to drive it. Once in a while, he lets me take it out and drive it by myself.

Also inside the warehouse were several large, metal shelves that resembled bookcases. The shelves contained various tools, and I noticed a hammer and several coffee cans filled with nails. Next to the shelving units were a few large, square pieces of plywood leaning against the wall.

Mr. Nelson then took us to see the irrigation building, which was basically an old, red barn. Like the warehouse, the barn had no floor, just hard-packed ground with a thin layer of hay. Parked inside the barn was an ancient, blue pickup truck covered with a film of chalky, gray dust. The truck looked like it hadn't moved in years.

There was also a very large, fifty-gallon, red drum labeled *WEED KILLER* in yellow lettering on the ground behind the truck. Like the truck, the big, red drum was covered with dust.

On the wall on the other side of the truck was a sickle with a long, wooden handle and a rusty blade. A sickle is a big tool, the length of a garden shovel. But instead of having a blade to dig a hole, it has a long, curved sword for cutting down tall grass and brush.

But the most impressive thing about the irrigation barn? An enormous, silver tank, three times the size of the truck. It sat next to the red barn like a giant, steel pill shining in the sun.

"This is a five-thousand gallon irrigation tank," Mr. Nelson explained, rapping on the metal with a bare knuckle. It made a metallic, hollow, echoing sound. "This is where all of the water is pumped from the ground and stored before it goes into the field. It's where we mix my special fertilizer with water. Each day, I add five gallons of liquid fertilizer to this tank, and only five gallons. The sprinklers are timed to go off at nine each morning," he added, "but sometimes, we have to manually turn them on. Especially during the hotter days when the plants need more water."

The fertilizer was stored in five gallon containers next to the red barn. The containers were made of yellow plastic and labeled *Warning! Incredible Ivy fertilizer. Handle with care!*

While we watched, Mr. Nelson poured one of the five gallon containers of fertilizer into the giant tank, which was exactly like pouring gasoline into a car.

"But what's so special about the ivy?" I asked. It was a question that I had been wanting to ask Mr. Nelson since the day before.

"Ah, yes," Mr. Nelson replied with a proud smile. "I've been working on this for several years. I've been able to successfully graft several types of plants together, including ivy, broccoli, asparagus, and spinach. What I've created is a hybrid plant that grows very fast. And it's one-hundred percent nutritionally complete. My incredible ivy contains all essential vitamins and minerals, and it's loaded with protein, carbohydrates, and fats that can sustain human life for months and months. Best of all, it's delicious."

"You mean," Jarvis said, his eyes widening, "you can *live* on this stuff?" He made a sweeping gesture with his arm that encompassed the field of red and green ivy. "I mean, if that's *all* I ate, I wouldn't have to eat *anything* else?"

Mr. Nelson nodded. "For a long time, yes," he replied. "Of course, you'd still have to drink water, as no human being can go for more than a few days without water. And eating the same food over and over would get boring, I'm afraid." His eyes lit up. "But think of the possibilities! If my ivy farm here in Prairie City is successful, we can duplicate plantations in other countries where food is badly needed. No one will ever have to starve again! My Incredible Ivy will go a long way toward eliminating world hunger."

Wow! I thought. *How exciting! Jarvis and I are part of a project that's going to make a huge difference in the world!*

"I've been working on this project—"

Mr. Nelson suddenly stopped speaking. His jaw fell. His eyes bulged, and he looked over my shoulder.

"Look out!" he screamed. *"Get down!"*

Mr. Nelson fell to his knees and covered his head

with his hands. Not knowing what to expect, the only thing Jarvis and I could do was get down and prepare for the worst . . . whatever that would be.

Jarvis and I did exactly what Mr. Nelson did: we fell to the ground and doubled over, covering the backs of our heads with our hands. After a few moments, when nothing happened, I slowly tilted my head to the side and opened my eyes. Mr. Nelson was doing the same, warily looking up into the sky.

"What is it?" Jarvis asked.

"A bumblebee," Mr. Nelson said. He sounded panicky. "He was coming right for us."

A bumblebee? I thought, unclasping my hands from

behind my head and tilting back to rest on my knees. I looked around. I didn't see any sign of a bee, and I wasn't that worried, anyway.

Mr. Nelson gets freaked out by an ordinary bee? I thought.

Mr. Nelson got to his feet. "I've been afraid of bumblebees ever since I was a little kid," he said. "Some people are terrified of spiders, and some people are afraid of snakes. For me, it's bees." Again, he looked around suspiciously. Not seeing any sign of the insect, his smile returned.

"I don't like snakes," Jarvis said as he stood, and as if he might see a snake at that very moment, he warily looked at the ground.

"I'm not afraid of anything," I said.

"Everybody's afraid of *something*," Jarvis said.

Jarvis was probably right. Everybody's afraid of something. But I'm not afraid of silly things like bees and snakes. I'm not even afraid of spiders, and both my mom and dad are terrified of them. Once, there was a spider in the bathtub, and my mom screamed like a baby. I went into the bathroom, scooped up the spider in my hand, and took him outside to let him go. It didn't bother me at all.

Mr. Nelson continued showing us around the farm. What was surprising to me was that the ivy didn't grow in a uniform fashion, like corn. Most farms have rows and rows and rows of plants, all growing in perfectly straight lines.

"All of the seeds were planted in rows," Mr. Nelson explained. "But the ivy grows in all sorts of different directions. Of course, the sunlight has a lot to do with it, but the vines finger out and grow as if each stem has a mind of its own. That's why it looks like a sea of plants. If you were to cut through all the ivy, you would see that the main stems are all in perfect rows."

And some of the vines had even spread out to cover the driveway and the yard. I had seen this before, in pictures of old homes. Most of these were in the southern part of the United States, where vines had grown up over telephone poles and chimneys and, sometimes, covered entire sides of houses.

"Next week," Mr. Nelson continued, "I'll begin cutting back the vines that are creeping too close to the buildings. But before I do that, there are other things that need to get done."

He explained the duties we would be performing. Mostly, we would be in charge of picking up things around the warehouse, cutting down weeds that had grown up, and putting fertilizer in the five-thousand gallon irrigation tank.

"Now, I've got some phone calls to make in my office," Mr. Nelson said. "You guys can start in the warehouse. All of the garbage cans need to be emptied into the big dumpster near the irrigation barn. Some of the cans are going to be heavy, so it'll take both of you. Oh," he said with a wink and a smile, "don't get into any trouble."

Jarvis and I laughed. After all: the things we were going to do were simple. We weren't going to do anything that could get us into trouble.

But, then again, we had no idea that trouble sometimes has a mind of its own. And in a few short minutes, *we* wouldn't find trouble . . . trouble would find *us*.

"He's kind of a quirky dude, don't you think?" Jarvis asked as we watched Mr. Nelson walk away.

"What do you mean?" I asked.

"You know," Jarvis said with a shrug. "Quirky. Odd. Kind of strange. I mean, he's nice enough and all, but he's—"

"—a little different," I finished.

"Yeah," said Jarvis. "I'm not being mean or anything."

"I know what you mean," I said. "My dad said the

same thing last night. He said that Mr. Nelson is brilliant. A genius, in fact. Dad said that a lot of really smart people are like that."

"Well, let's get to work," Jarvis said. "We've got lots to do."

"Yeah," I replied. "Where do you want to start?"

"Let's do the heaviest stuff first," Jarvis suggested. "Let's get that out of the way, so we don't have to think about it."

That sounded like a good idea, so we started out toward the warehouse. It was like walking on an island in the middle of a sea of vines of red and green ivy. In many places, the vines had fingered into the driveway where we walked, and I remembered what Mr. Nelson had told us about how the ivy grows very fast, and that next week, he'd have to start pruning them back to keep them from covering the driveway. I hoped that we'd get to help with that, too.

At the warehouse, we found a bunch of large aluminum garbage cans that needed to be emptied. Most of them contained what appeared to be compost: dark gobs of rotting vegetation, leaves, and stems. Add to that some old newspapers, plastic bags, cups, and other assorted pieces of trash. The stench was heavy, thick, and pungent. Much of the paper and vegetation were wet, too, making the cans very heavy. I tried to lift one on my own, but I could barely get it off the ground.

"Careful, careful," Jarvis said. "Don't hurt yourself. I'll help."

Jarvis grabbed the handle on one side of the garbage can, and I grabbed the other. That made it easier. It was still heavy, but we were able to lift it off the ground and walk with it.

"Good thing we don't have to carry this thing very far," I said, nodding toward the big black dumpster on the other side of the parking lot, next to the red irrigation barn.

"Yeah, but it's going to take all of our strength to lift it up and empty it out," Jarvis said.

"I hope there aren't too many—"

Without warning, something wrapped around my ankle. I stumbled forward and tried to free my foot, but whatever had hold of me wasn't going to let go. Before I could do anything, I was falling forward, out of control, my ankle still held firmly by something that had seized it, holding tightly, locked around it.

In a single, lightning-fast motion, I let go of the garbage can and fell forward. I was able to get both arms in front of me, so I didn't land flat on my face, but my elbows took the blow on the hard-packed dirt. The wind exploded from my chest, and the garbage can tumbled over, spewing its contents of mulch and papers and junk.

"Whoa, whoa," Jarvis exclaimed as he rushed to me and knelt down. "Are you okay?"

I rolled to my side, fighting to catch my breath.

"I . . . I think so," I said, holding a hand to my chest

and gasping.

"Sorry about that," Jarvis said. "It happened so fast, there was nothing I could do to help you."

Jarvis reached down with his right hand, and I took it with my left. He pulled and helped me up, and I stood for a moment, bending over, clutching my chest, still trying to catch my breath.

Jarvis bent down and reached for something. "Here," he said. "You tripped on this." He stood up, holding an old, frayed rope. "This is what caught your foot and tripped you up."

I tried to laugh, but my chest hurt. I still couldn't catch my breath. It seemed strange that I had been clumsy enough to trip over an old rope.

Then again, I reminded myself that I could've been hurt. I'd have to be more careful. I didn't want to do anything that would cause me to not be able to work. Then, I wouldn't earn any money. Which, of course, meant that I wouldn't be able to buy my bicycle.

After I caught my breath, we picked up all of the garbage that spilled from the can and returned to the task of hauling it across the field. Despite the can's weight, we managed to lift it up and empty it into the big dumpster near the irrigation building. We spent the next hour doing this, dragging garbage cans across the field, emptying them, returning to the warehouse for more. When we had emptied the last one and were returning it to the warehouse, Mr. Nelson appeared once again.

"All of the garbage cans are empty," Jarvis said to him.

Mr. Nelson smiled, clearly pleased. "Nice work," he said. "Follow me, and I'll show you what's next."

He led us around the warehouse toward the edge of the field. Here, looking straight ahead and to the left of us, red and green ivy seemed to grow as far as the eye could see. To the right was the fence line. Ivy grew right up to it, climbing the fence in many places. In some spots, it looked like it was crawling over the fence, as if it was looking for an escape route.

Like red and green snakes in a cage, trying to find a way out, I thought.

Near the fence, where the land had been cleared and no ivy was growing, there were several large piles of brush.

Mr. Nelson looked at his watch. "It's getting a little late today," he said, "but tomorrow, I'd like you to move all of this brush to the big clearing on the other side of the warehouse. I've got a large chipping machine that'll grind up all of the branches, and we can recycle the little wood chips."

"That'll be cool!" Jarvis said. "I've never used a wood chipper before."

37

Mr. Nelson shook his head. "And you're not going to," he replied. "It's a little too dangerous for you guys. I'm going to have some of my other workers take care of that after the weekend. But it'll be a big help for you guys to move the brush pile closer to where we'll be grinding them up."

"Rats," Jarvis said under his breath.

"For now, though," Mr. Nelson continued, "I'm going to have you clean the windows of the warehouse, both inside and out. That'll take you a little while, and when you're done, you can go home. But be ready to put in a full day tomorrow, as there's still a lot of work that'll need to get done before the regular crew comes back on Monday."

That night, I had no trouble getting to sleep. Working most of the afternoon had worn me out, and I think I crashed out as soon as my head hit the pillow.

But I had dreams. I dreamed of working with Jarvis at *Incredible Ivy*. I dreamed of Mr. Nelson, counting out money as he handed it to me, thanking me for a job well done. I dreamed of my new bicycle, riding it through fields and forests, blazing down paths and making my own trails.

But I didn't have any nightmares.

None at all.

No, the horrifying nightmares would come later.

The problem was, when the nightmares *did* come,

I wouldn't be sleeping, and I wouldn't be dreaming. They wouldn't be the visions of my imagination, and they wouldn't go away if I wished myself awake.

The nightmares would be *real*.

7

My clock radio beside my bed awoke me at exactly 6 AM, blaring some crazy song. The intrusive sound caused my entire body to tense, and I rolled to my side and slapped frantically at the clock until I found the button. Finally, the music stopped, and I flopped lazily onto my back with my eyes closed, my head resting on the soft pillow.

I sighed. *Who on earth gets up at this hour on a Saturday morning?* I wondered, determined to go back to sleep.

Then, my head cleared. I remembered my job at

Incredible Ivy and snapped up in bed.

Work day! I thought. *Jarvis and I are working at* Incredible Ivy *today. We have to be there early to get started!*

I forgot all about being tired as I swept my legs to the side, slipped off the bed, and stood. I walked to my bedroom window, drew back the curtain with my index finger, and peered outside.

In the east, the sun was just beginning to rise. The sky was a beautiful mixture of orange, yellow, pink, and red. It was going to be a beautiful day.

I went into the kitchen. Since it was Saturday, Mom and Dad were sleeping in. I poured myself a bowl of cereal and made a couple slices of toast. Then, I returned to my bedroom, changed into some old clothing, and left a note for Mom and Dad. Although they knew I'd be up early and gone, I left them a note anyway, telling them that I wasn't sure if I'd be home for lunch or not. I hoped so, because I was sure that I would be hungry by then, and I didn't know if Mr. Nelson had any food. Then, as an afterthought, I made two sandwiches and put them in a paper bag with two apples, two bananas, and two candy bars.

Just in case, I thought. *If we have to eat lunch on the fly, this will be enough for Jarvis and me.*

I stuffed the paper lunch sack into my backpack, slung it over my shoulder, and found my bike helmet. I slipped quietly out the front door, closing it slowly behind me. I hadn't taken two steps onto the porch when I heard a voice.

"I thought you were going to sleep all day," I heard, instantly recognizing Jarvis's voice. I looked up to see him seated on his bicycle on the sidewalk, hands on the handlebars, leaning forward, waiting.

I smiled. "How long have you been here?" I asked.

"Just got here," he replied. "It's going to be a great day."

I hustled to the garage and retrieved my bike, leaping on it as I rolled down the driveway toward Jarvis.

"What's in the backpack?" Jarvis asked as we started out.

"I brought lunch for us, just in case," I replied. "Just a couple of sandwiches, apples, bananas, and candy bars."

"Good thinking," Jarvis said. "I hadn't thought about that. We're probably going to get pretty hungry."

In minutes, we were at the locked, green gate. The sun had risen, and dawn's vibrant, early morning colors had given way to a beautiful, blue sky. On the other side of the fence was an ocean of red and green ivy, motionless in the early morning stillness. The leaves and stems were shiny and wet, covered with a layer of cool dew.

And I don't know why, but I was suddenly struck with a feeling of horror, a tinge of dread that was so strong that I wanted to turn my bike around and go home, pedaling as fast as I could. Everything just seemed too *perfect*, too *right*.

"Kayla?" Jarvis asked. "What's wrong? You look like you've seen a ghost."

I smiled, shaking away my fears. "Nothing," I replied, suddenly feeling very silly. "I just can't wait to get started."

Mr. Nelson showed up a few minutes later in his white truck.

"Sorry I'm a few minutes late," he said, opening the driver's side door and stepping out. "Mrs. Nelson needed me to take out the trash, and then I had to stop by the gas station and fill up my truck."

He unlocked the gate, pushed it open, and returned to his vehicle. "Throw your bikes in the back," he said. "I'll give you guys a ride up the driveway."

Jarvis and I did as he instructed, then climbed into the cab of the truck. I slipped off my backpack and put it on my lap.

"Looks like it's going to be a nice day," Mr. Nelson said.

"It sure does," Jarvis said.

As the truck bumped along, I couldn't help but notice the many vines stretching out over the narrow driveway, vines that hadn't been there last night when we left. They were creeping across the gravel, lying in wait like sleeping snakes in the morning sun.

Again, I was struck with that feeling of stark, white fear, that gnawing sensation of dark dread, but I didn't say anything.

Maybe I *should* have. Maybe I *should* have told Mr. Nelson and Jarvis that I had a feeling that something was wrong.

But no. Looking back, they probably would've laughed at me. They would've said that I had an overactive imagination.

Instead, this is what I said:

"It looks like the ivy grew a little bit since yesterday."

Mr. Nelson nodded. "They *do* grow a little during the nighttime hours," he replied. "But mostly," he continued, "they grow during the day, when the sun is shining." He pointed up into the sky, at the yellow ball slowly rising in the east. "And they'll probably do a lot of growing today," he finished.

I looked out the window, at the sea of red and green ivy passing by as the white truck ambled up the driveway, toward the warehouse and office of *Incredible Ivy*. Then, I pulled out my phone from my back pocket and looked at the time.

6:45 AM.

I didn't know it then, of course, but the countdown

to our nightmare had already begun . . . and there was no way to turn back the clock.

Mr. Nelson parked the truck in front of his office, and the three of us got out. Jarvis and I took our bikes out of the back of the truck and leaned them against the wall near the office door. I looped my backpack and helmet over the handlebars.

"Isn't there anyone else here?" Jarvis asked as he looked around.

"It's Saturday," Mr. Nelson replied. "Everyone else has the day off. They'll come back on Monday, which means that there's plenty of work for both of you to do."

"That's fine with me," I replied. "I'm ready to work."

"Me, too," Jarvis echoed.

"Where do we start?" I asked.

"Jarvis," Mr. Nelson said, "I'll need you to pour the five gallons of fertilizer into the irrigation tank before the sprinklers come on at nine. Kayla, you come with me, and I'll show you where I keep more cleaning supplies. Did either one of you bring a pair of gloves?"

I looked at Jarvis, and he looked at me. Both of us shook our heads.

"Sorry," I said sheepishly. "I guess we didn't think of that."

"No matter," Mr. Nelson said. "I've got plenty. Come on."

Jarvis began walking in the opposite direction toward the barn and the huge, silver irrigation tank, and I followed Mr. Nelson as he walked toward his office. By now, the day was beginning to get warm as the sun rose higher in the sky.

"It's going to be a great day," Mr. Nelson said. "I'm glad you two are able to work this weekend. There's a lot that needs to get done."

Mr. Nelson pulled a wad of keys from his pocket, and then he turned and looked at Jarvis, who was making his way toward the irrigation tank.

"On second thought," Mr. Nelson said, "I'm going to

48

have him wait before filling the irrigation tank. He really should be wearing gloves when he handles the liquid fertilizer."

Mr. Nelson raised both of his hands and cupped them around his mouth.

"Jarvis!" he called out. "Don't put the fertilizer in the irrigation tank. You can do it after I get you some gloves!"

In the distance, I saw Jarvis turn and look at us. He paused for a moment and then waved.

"He seems like a nice kid," Mr. Nelson said as he inserted a key into the lock, turned it, and opened the door to his office.

"He is," I said. "I've known him for a long time. He's a good friend and a hard worker."

I followed Mr. Nelson into his office. He strode to a large cabinet on the far wall and opened the door. Inside were several shelves filled with cleaning supplies and bottles containing other fluids. There were also several pairs of leather gloves. He grabbed two pairs and held them up.

"These are going to be a little big for you and Jarvis," he said, "but they'll keep your hands protected." He handed both pairs to me. "Take one pair to Jarvis, and make sure he wears them all day. You, too."

And he was right about the gloves being too big. I

tried mine, and they looked like baseball mitts on my hands. Oh well. They would keep my hands from getting scuffed and scraped, and that was all that mattered.

"I keep all of the cleaning supplies in here," Mr. Nelson said, "along with old rags and brushes. You'll need these when you get around to cleaning the office windows and some other parts of the warehouse. Now, I've got to run some errands, so I'll leave the door to my office unlocked, so you can come in here and get supplies as you need them."

"Okay," I said.

Mr. Nelson looked at his watch. "If I leave now, I can get to the hardware store right when it opens." He looked at me. "Before you help Jarvis with the brush piles, I want you to pour the five gallons of fertilizer into the irrigation tank. Be sure to wear your gloves, and don't get any of the liquid on your skin."

I nodded. "Okay," I replied.

I followed Mr. Nelson out of his office and watched him drive off. I knew I was going to really like working at *Incredible Ivy*. Mr. Nelson treated me like a grown-up, like a real employee. I liked that a lot.

And I also liked the fact that I was going to earn money for my bicycle.

Maybe, I thought, *if I show Mr. Nelson that I'm a really good worker, he'll hire me to do even more work. Then,*

I can earn even more *money. Maybe I can even—*

My thought was stopped by a sudden, bloodcurdling scream that echoed over the ocean of red and green ivy. The sound sent a shiver down my back for two reasons. Number one, it was obviously a cry of deep, horrible pain.

And number two?

I knew who was screaming.

Jarvis.

I had no idea what was wrong, but I knew Jarvis needed help, and fast. I took off at a sprint, running as fast as my legs would carry me across the hard-packed ground. I turned my head from side to side, eyes searching left and right.

Where is he?!?! I thought. *What's happened?*

Jarvis had stopped screaming, but I still didn't see him anywhere.

"Jarvis?!?!" I shouted. *"Where are you?!?! Are you okay?!?!"*

"Over here!" Jarvis called out, and I could still hear the fear in his voice. It was coming from the far side of the warehouse, and I altered my course and ran to help him.

When I rounded the corner, I saw Jarvis against the wall of the warehouse. He was pinned there as if blown by a strong wind. His palms were flat on the wall, his eyes were focused downward, gazing at something on the ground, and his mouth was open in a silent scream of terror.

"What is it?!?!" I asked, still running toward him.

"It's after me!" Jarvis shrieked. *"It's after me! It's trying to kill me!"*

I slowed as I drew closer, wary of whatever was frightening Jarvis. Of course, it never came to my mind that the ivy was attacking him; that was just too crazy, too unbelievable.

And I was right, of course.

As I approached, I searched the ground in front of Jarvis until I saw the threat:

A garter snake.

Are you kidding me? I thought.

The snake was black with a yellow stripe down its back, and it wasn't even very big: probably no longer than my arm.

"You're afraid of *that?*" I said, pointing at the snake as I stood over it.

"He came after me!" Jarvis shouted.

"Snakes don't chase people!" I insisted. "Especially garter snakes. They don't even have teeth!"

"I'm telling you," Jarvis said, still pressed against the wall of the warehouse. "He attacked me. He was trying to bite."

I reach down and picked up the snake. He really was very cool-looking, squirming in my hand, his forked tongue slipping in and out, in and out.

"See?" I said. "He's harmless. You probably scared him more than he scared you."

"Yeah," Jarvis said, "but you're wearing gloves."

"That doesn't matter," I said. "He's not going to bite me."

Jarvis covered his eyes. "Get rid of him," he said. "I never want to see him again."

I turned and carried the snake to the fence, where I knelt down and placed the reptile on the ground.

"Bye-bye," I said. "Go eat some grasshoppers or something. Have a nice life." I watched him slither away into the brush, where he vanished.

In my left hand, I was still carrying the pair of gloves for Jarvis, and I took them to him. He had finally calmed down a little and was no longer plastered against the wall of the warehouse.

"Here," I said, handing him the gloves. "Put these

on. Mr. Nelson says we should wear them while we're working."

Jarvis slipped on the gloves. Like the ones I had on, they were too big for him, too.

"Let's get busy," I said. "We have a lot of work to do."

Little by little, we began hauling the stacks of dead branches to the field on the other side of the warehouse. After a few minutes, I remembered that Mr. Nelson had asked me to pour the five gallons of fertilizer into the irrigation tank, so I left Jarvis to continue working at the brush pile while I completed the task. When I returned, he was still busy, and we worked together for the next hour.

All the while, I kept glancing over my shoulder, staring out over the vast field of green and red ivy. I just couldn't shake the feeling that we were being watched, and I expected to see someone standing in the field, looking back at me. I saw no one, and I tried to keep my mind on my work. Still, I felt a little nervous, and I couldn't help it.

Just as we finished moving the brush piles, the sprinkler system kicked on. A network of pipes and tubes began spraying water all over the ivy.

I pulled my phone from my back pocket. It was exactly 9 AM, the time that Mr. Nelson said the sprinklers were set to turn on.

"What's our next job?" Jarvis asked.

"Mr. Nelson wants us to clean all of the windows in the main office, inside and out," I replied. "That's probably going to take us the rest of the day."

We started walking toward the main office, and I noticed Jarvis looking back over his shoulder.

"What's wrong?" I asked, glancing over my own shoulder to see the field of red and green ivy glistening in the sun.

"Oh, nothing," Jarvis replied. "It's just—"

Jarvis paused in mid-sentence, as if he didn't know what to say.

"What?" I prodded. "What's the matter?"

"Well, I know it's silly," he said. "But I can't help but feel that the ivy seems to be growing really fast."

I stopped, and Jarvis did the same. We turned and looked out over the ocean of ivy.

"You know," I said, "I had the same feeling earlier. But it's just my imagination. Yours, too. Mr. Nelson said that the ivy grows faster in the sun, remember?"

"I know," Jarvis answered. "But I guess I—"

"Forget about it," I said. I turned and began walking toward the main office. Jarvis followed, but he continued talking.

"I can't put my finger on it," he continued, "but something just doesn't seem right. I don't know what it is."

"I just think that your imagination is—"

Now, it was my turn to stop speaking in mid-sentence. A movement had caught my attention, and I glanced up.

I stopped walking.

Jarvis stopped walking.

We both stared.

"That's impossible," Jarvis whispered. His voice trembled with fear.

Ahead of us, vines of red and green ivy were climbing up the sides of the warehouse, moving back and forth, squirming like snakes, scaling the building!

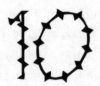

They're alive, I thought. *I mean, of course they're alive, because they're plants. But now they've become animated, like reptiles. Like snakes.*

In a panic, I had already reached for my phone and was dialing Mr. Nelson's number. He said to call if there was an emergency. Well, if this wasn't an emergency, I didn't know what was.

"Who are you calling?" Jarvis asked. I could still hear the terror in his voice. Neither of us could tear our eyes away from the horrific scene unfolding.

"Mr. Nelson," I replied. "He has to know about this. Something is really, really wrong."

"Look at them move," Jarvis said, pointing. "They're moving just like snakes, wiggling just like worms. How can they do that?"

Holding the phone to my ear, I shook my head. "I don't know," I replied to Jarvis. "But something's really wrong. Mr. Nelson needs to know about it."

The phone rang several times in my ear and then went to his message service. After the beep, I spoke.

"Mr. Nelson, this is Kayla Blaisdale. There's something really strange going on and—"

—*and what?* I thought. *What am I going to tell him? That the vines were alive, that the ivy was trying to climb up the building all by itself? He would probably think that I was off my rocker.*

But I *hadn't* gone crazy. I knew what I was seeing, and so did Jarvis. We were both seeing the same thing: vines of red and green ivy were climbing up the building, slithering up the wall under their own power.

"—and the ivy has come to life," I continued. "What I mean to say is that it's moving around like snakes. We're watching some vines try to climb up the side of the warehouse right now."

"Tell him that they've reached the roof!" Jarvis said excitedly.

Still speaking into the phone, I continued. "The ivy has climbed all the way up the side of the warehouse and is now slithering up onto the roof," I said. "It's the craziest thing I have—"

Suddenly, I was yanked off my feet. My phone went flying, and I had to use both arms to block my fall. Still, I hit the ground really hard.

Unhurt but confused, I rolled to my side and sat up. However, when I tried to stand, I couldn't.

A vine of red ivy had wrapped itself tightly around my left ankle!

For a moment, I couldn't do anything but stare. Then, the vine encircled both of my ankles, and as I watched, it was slowly wrapping itself more and more, pulling tighter and tighter.

"Jarvis!" I shrieked. *"Jarvis! Help me!"*

Jarvis fell to his knees and grabbed the vine around my ankles. He frantically pulled at it, unwrapping the plant as it squirmed in his hands. Finally, I was able to pull both feet free.

I quickly rolled to my knees and then pushed myself

up. At my feet, the vine was still squiggling and squirming, trying to reach my feet. As I took a step back, Jarvis grabbed my forearm and held tightly. With his other arm, he pointed out across the field.

"Look!" he said.

Before us was the vast ocean of red and green ivy. Wet from the sprinklers, they shined brightly, glossy and smooth in the morning sun.

And they were moving! All of the vines were slowly weaving in and out, back and forth, among each other, over and down, left and right.

"I'm not seeing this," I said. "This isn't happening."

"Oh, yes it is," Jarvis replied. "I'm seeing the same thing you are."

Right then, I wanted to be anywhere else. I didn't care where it was, but I didn't want to be at the farm. I didn't want to be at *Incredible Ivy*. I didn't care about the job; I didn't care about the money. I didn't even care about my bicycle at that point. I just wanted to get away. I wanted to be safe. I wanted to be anywhere away from the field of live ivy.

"We've got to get somewhere safe until Mr. Nelson gets back!" I said. "We've got to get inside!"

We turned and began running toward the warehouse, and it was then that I noticed that not only were the vines in the field alive, but many of them were now spreading out, covering the ground, slithering over the driveway and other areas that hadn't been planted. In fact, we had to leap over a few of them while we ran. As we did, several of them tried to rise up, and a couple of them actually touched my legs. Every time that happened, I cringed, but none of the plants were able to get a grip and take hold.

"Almost there!" Jarvis shouted as we ran.

Ahead of us, the warehouse loomed large. More vines were now making their way up the side of the building, and a number of them had reached the roof. They were hanging down from the eaves, swaying back and forth like live electrical wires. A couple of them hung in front of the warehouse door.

Jarvis was ahead of me, and he bolted to the door, grabbing the handle. He pushed the door open, but not before a vine succeeded in looping beneath his left arm. For a moment, I thought he was caught, but he was able to quickly pull free.

But he wasn't going to be that lucky.

Just then, another vine came down from above, thick and green, as big around as a garden hose. It wrapped around his neck and quickly tightened.

This time, Jarvis didn't have a chance. His eyes bulged, and he tried to let out a scream, but no sound came out. His hands flew up to the vine around his neck, and he struggled madly to pull the plant away.

But it was too late. The vine was too strong; Jarvis was too slow. In the next instant, the vine had yanked him off the ground by his neck!

Jarvis kicked madly with both legs, but his effort did nothing. He had been pulled off the ground, and although he had a grip on the vine with both hands, the ivy still remained tightly wound around his neck. His face was turning blue, and his eyes were bulging. He was choking!

I didn't know what to do. I knew I had to do *something*, but what? I couldn't just grab hold of his waist and try to pull him free, as I was sure that would just make things worse. The vine would choke him even more. But the plant had pulled him several inches off the ground, and the ivy around his neck had cut off his air supply. Jarvis couldn't breathe.

And if he couldn't breathe . . . .

His right hand suddenly flew down and plunged into his pocket. Out came his red-handled pocket knife, but he lost his grip, and the tool fell to the ground.

I dove and grabbed the knife. Rolling it over in my hands, I searched among the folded tools and quickly found the largest blade, unfolded it, and stood. Once again, Jarvis had both hands at his neck, trying to pull the vine away.

Standing on my tiptoes, I reached up with the knife and held the sharp edge of the blade against the vine. Using a back and forth sawing motion, I sliced at the ivy behind his neck. All the while, Jarvis made horrible gurgling and coughing sounds. I knew that if I didn't cut the vine quickly, he was going to pass out due to lack of air.

Redoubling my efforts, I moved the blade faster and faster. The vine was thick and tough, but the blade was doing its job.

Halfway through.

Jarvis struggled and kicked.

I continued with the knife, furiously cutting back and forth at the vine, back and forth . . . .

Jarvis's whole body stiffened and tightened.

Three quarters of the way through the vine—

Jarvis kicked violently, but his legs were suspended

in air. His efforts were in vain.

Then, the knife blade finished its job. The vine severed. In one sudden movement, Jarvis fell to the ground. His legs couldn't support him, and he tumbled over. The vine was still wrapped around his neck, his hands still gripping the plant.

I folded the knife blade into its handle and stuffed it into my front pocket. Then, I fell to my knees and pulled at the remaining piece of ivy that was still wrapped around Jarvis's neck. It easily came away, now that it had been cut away. I tossed it to the ground where it landed and twitched like a dying animal.

Jarvis was coughing and gasping, finding it difficult to catch his breath. I grabbed his hand and pulled him to his feet.

"Inside!" I shouted. *"We have to get into the warehouse!"*

Jarvis was still a little dazed, so I gave him a push through the door. He stumbled and fell, but there was nothing I could do about that. Besides: at least he was in the warehouse. At least he was safe.

Above me, more vines were reaching down from the roof, dangling and squirming. I quickly ducked beneath them and darted through the door, slamming it closed behind me.

By now, Jarvis was on his knees. He had one hand

around his neck and one on his chest, breathing deeply, heaving, his lungs sucking in air.

"Thank . . . thank you," he wheezed.

"Are you okay?" I asked. It was a silly question, but I didn't know what else to say. My best friend had nearly choked to death. Things like that don't happen every day.

Jarvis nodded. "I . . . I . . . thi . . . I think so," he stammered. "Man! When I dropped my knife, I thought that was the end of me! I'm sure glad you were there."

"I'm glad, too," I said as I dug into my front pocket. "Here," I said, producing his pocket knife. I held it out to him, and he took it.

"I'm sure glad I bought this when I did," Jarvis said, inspecting the knife for a moment before he stuffed it into his pocket. "It helped you save my life."

I shuddered, realizing that if Jarvis hadn't had his pocket knife, there wouldn't have been anything I could have done to save him. The vine would have strangled him.

I took a step toward the window and gazed outside. Jarvis joined me, and we just stared.

That same creeping horror that I'd felt earlier in the day returned. It started as a cold tingle, but quickly turned into an overwhelming chill. My skin broke out in goose flesh, and the tiny hairs on my arms stood up.

The entire field was a mass of tangled ivy. The sprinklers continued spraying, and the fine mist of water shined in the sun, creating colorful rainbows. But all of the vines had come alive, twisting and turning, roiling and boiling, each one moving independently, on its own.

They're alive, I thought. *They're alive. And they're deadly.* It was truly one of the scariest moments of my life.

"At least we're inside," Jarvis said quietly. "We'll be safe in here. We'll be safe until Mr. Nelson returns."

Oh, how I wished Jarvis was right. At the time, I believed him. I really thought that we would be safe inside the warehouse. I really thought that Mr. Nelson would be returning at any moment, and our nightmare would be over.

Wrong.

The worst hadn't even happened yet . . . but it was about to.

Knowing we were safe (or at least *thinking* we were safe at the time), we stood at the window and stared out over the field for several minutes. I found it impossible to take my eyes away. Vines continued to spread and grow right before our eyes, slithering across the driveway, crisscrossing one another like red and green snakes with leaves. Vines hung from above and dangled from the roof of the warehouse, and several stalks tapped lightly at the window. They were only inches from our faces.

"Have you ever heard of anything like this before?"

Jarvis asked quietly.

I shook my head. "Nothing like this," I said. "Something is really, really wrong."

"I sure hope Mr. Nelson gets back quick," Jarvis said. "He'll know what to do."

"I hope so, too," I agreed. "Until then, there's nothing we can do but wait. At least we're safe in here."

"Look at that!" Jarvis suddenly exclaimed, pointing out the window.

Not far away, one of the vines had wrapped itself around a garden shovel. The plant had raised the shovel into the air and was waving it back and forth like a toy. While we watched, the vine effortlessly snapped the shovel in two. I couldn't help but think about the vine that had wrapped itself around Jarvis's neck. Once again, I realized how lucky he'd been.

Seeing how easily the vine had snapped the shovel, Jarvis raised his right hand and gently stroked his neck. "Wow," he said quietly. "I was luckier than I thought."

"I wonder if Mr. Nelson knows about this," I said. "I wonder if he's aware that his ivy is alive."

"And dangerous," Jarvis added.

"Probably not," I replied, answering my own question. "He probably has no idea. Otherwise, he would never have left us alone. Who would leave two kids alone with killer plants?"

Again, we were silent, staring out the window, watching the vines crawl over one another, a vast ocean of red and green wires, twisting and turning about.

"Well," Jarvis said, "there's nothing we can do about it except wait. We have to stay put until Mr. Nelson comes back."

I reached into my back pocket to retrieve my phone. I was going to make another phone call to Mr. Nelson to see if he would answer. If he didn't, I'd call Mom and Dad. And if *they* didn't answer, I would seriously consider calling the police.

However, in all the excitement, I'd forgotten one important thing:

"Oh, no!" I suddenly exclaimed.

"What?" Jarvis asked, turning to look at me.

"My phone!" I replied. "It was knocked out of my hand when I fell!"

We looked out the window again, and Jarvis spotted my phone in the driveway among a tangle of plants.

"There it is," he said, "I can see it right there, on the ground in the driveway."

"Tell me you brought your phone," I said.

Jarvis shook his head. "Nope. My sister and I share one phone, and this is her day to have it."

I was really bummed out. Now, if anyone tried to return my phone calls, I'd never know.

"Hey," Jarvis said, sensing my frustration. "Don't worry. You left a message with Mr. Nelson. I'm sure he got it, and he'll be here any minute. We're going to be fine."

Jarvis was right. We had done everything we could. We were in a very serious, dangerous situation, but as long as we remained in the warehouse, we would be safe. We would be okay.

All that changed when we heard a noise behind us.

Actually, there were *two* sounds. There was a loud, metallic popping sound, followed by a muffled, rattling crash, like something had fallen to the floor.

Jarvis and I flinched and turned. At first, we didn't see anything.

I leaned closer to Jarvis, placing my mouth next to his ear. *"What was that?"* I whispered.

Jarvis shook his head. *"I don't know,"* he whispered back. Then, he slowly raised his arm and pointed. *"It sounded like it came from over there."*

That creeping feeling of horror returned. It started in my toes and went up through my ankles, into my legs, up through my waist and tummy, filled my chest, and finally reached my head. My entire body tensed, and I felt dizzy. Still, my eyes continued searching inside the warehouse. The green and yellow tractor was parked against the far wall, as if sleeping. Other than that, the only other things in the warehouse were a few bare shelves and several coils of green hoses hanging on the walls.

Cautiously, Jarvis took a step forward.

"Where are you going?" I asked quietly.

"I think the noise came from over there," Jarvis said, pointing once again. "Let's go find out what it is."

"Let's not," I said, shaking my head. "Let's stay right here and—"

I was interrupted by yet another metallic popping sound and another rattling crash. This time, we saw something move, and we turned our heads in time to see a large, square piece of metal fall from the warehouse wall. It crashed to the floor, bounced a couple of times, and stopped.

But that didn't hold our attention for long.

Something in the wall was moving.

Jarvis froze.

I froze.

"I can't believe this is happening," Jarvis said in a voice that was just above a whisper. *"This is totally crazy."*

Two twisting stalks of ivy, one red and one green, were coming into the warehouse through the wall! They had succeeded in popping off the cover of the air vent, and now they were coming to get us!

If I'd been terrified before, it was nothing *close* to what I was now feeling. I thought that since we were in the warehouse, we'd be safe. I thought we'd found a way to escape the attacking plants.

Think again.

For a moment, Jarvis and I just stood there, frozen in fear, watching the ivy as it dangled through the square opening in the wall. It was strange, but the plants behaved as if they were looking around, as if they had eyes, as if they were seeking us out. I knew that it wasn't possible, that plants simply don't behave like wild animals.

But then again, I couldn't be sure. At that moment, I would've believed just about anything.

Another movement caught our attention, and we turned to see even more vines coming through another hole in the wall on the other side of the warehouse.

"We've gotta get outta here!" I said.

"Yeah," Jarvis agreed, "but where are we gonna go? We can't go outside, because the place is crawling with those plants."

Frantically, I looked around the warehouse. I didn't know what I was looking for, but I knew we needed to find some way to defend ourselves. I knew that Jarvis still had his pocket knife, but that might not do a lot of good if we were up against more than one or two vines.

Then, I spotted something.

That might work! I thought as my head turned from side to side, still scanning the warehouse. *If there was only—*

"There!" I suddenly exclaimed, so loudly that it surprised Jarvis, and he jumped.

"What?" Jarvis said.

"I have an idea!" I said, and I shot one more quick glance out the window to see if Mr. Nelson's truck was in sight. I was hoping that it was, because then it would be only a matter of time before we'd be rescued. But when I didn't see him, I knew we had to act.

"What?" Jarvis repeated, more insistent this time. "What's your idea?"

"There's a hammer and some coffee cans with nails on that shelf over there," I pointed. "Go get those." Then, I pointed to the sheets of plywood leaning against the wall. "If we hurry, we can board up the holes before the vines get through all the way!"

"There's not enough time!" Jarvis said.

"It's our only chance!" I insisted. "Mr. Nelson's not here yet, and we have to do something to stop those things from getting inside!"

Quickly, we got to work. I grabbed a big piece of plywood. The edges were rough against my bare skin, but at least the wood wasn't heavy, and I didn't have to carry it very far.

Jarvis raced to the shelf and grabbed the can of nails and the hammer, and we hurried to the first hole in the wall. A couple of strands of ivy had made it through, and he began pounding the stem with the hammer. With every blow, the plant recoiled.

I covered the hole with the piece of plywood, pressing it with both hands to hold it in place.

"There!" I said. "Now, nail it to the wall! Hurry, before those things in the wall try to push it away!"

Jarvis got to work. He accidentally dropped the first

nail and then grabbed another. Quickly, he pounded the nail through the plywood and into the wall. He repeated this seven or eight times with more nails, going all around the side of the plywood.

Meanwhile, I was keeping an eye on the other hole, where still more vines were coming through. One of them had already reached the floor and was crawling along, squirming like a lizard.

"Okay, one more," I said, removing my hands from the plywood. The wood held, and I quickly turned, raced to the other side of the warehouse, grabbed another piece of plywood, and carried it to the remaining hole in the wall. Jarvis joined me, and he kicked at the long, green vine that was crawling along the floor. The plant behaved like a snake, and in my mind, I could hear it hissing, like it was preparing to strike. A couple smaller vines were slowly making their way through the vent hole.

"I can't put the plywood over the hole until that vine is out of the way!" I said.

Dropping the hammer and the can of nails, Jarvis dug into his pocket and pulled out his knife. He unfolded the blade and bravely raced to the hole. Quickly, he grabbed the vine and began cutting at it with his knife. In seconds, he had severed the plant, and a long section fell to the floor. It gave several twitches, then stopped moving.

"There!" Jarvis said, folding the blade and returning

his knife to his pocket. "Hurry! Put that piece of plywood over the hole, and I'll nail it to the wall!"

Quickly, Jarvis got to work, furiously nailing the board to the wall. He fumbled with the nails a few times, but it didn't take him long to complete the task. Finally, he was done, and we both stepped back.

In the wall, we could hear the vines trying to push at the plywood, but the board held.

Then, I quickly snapped my head around, searching for more vents that might have popped open. I didn't see any, and I breathed a sigh of relief.

"Mr. Nelson has got to be back soon," I said, moving through the warehouse to the window. Jarvis followed, and we stared off into the distance, over the mass of tangled green and red ivy that was still twisting and turning about, more alive than ever.

"Maybe his phone battery is out of juice," Jarvis said. "Or maybe he doesn't have his phone on. Maybe he didn't get your message."

I didn't like that thought, but Jarvis was right. It was very possible that Mr. Nelson didn't have his phone on, or maybe the battery was dead. He could be at the hardware store right now, chatting with some friends, completely unaware of the horror taking place at his farm.

So, for the time being, we were completely alone, on our own.

Unless—

"I have another idea," I said.

"What's that?" Jarvis asked.

"My phone is out there on the ground," I said. "It doesn't look like the vines can move very fast. If I hurry, I'll bet I'd be able to get to my phone and get back here without any of the plants having time to get hold of me."

Jarvis thought about this.

"That's a good idea," he said, "but I'm a faster runner than you are. I'll go. I'll go grab the phone and bring it back here."

I looked at Jarvis, and he looked at me. I knew he was wondering the same thing that I was.

Was it the right thing to do?

I didn't know. But I knew that we couldn't just stay in the warehouse and wait for help that might not arrive. By then, it might be too late. There was no telling what the ivy was capable of doing.

"I'll go," Jarvis repeated. "I'm fast, and I can outrun the ivy. Besides," he continued, digging into his pocket and pulling out his pocket knife. "I have my knife. If I get in trouble, I can use it." He returned the knife to his pocket and looked outside.

"Are you sure about this?" I asked.

"It'll be a cinch," he replied. "I can run faster than a speeding bullet."

84

I thought about how fast a bullet moves, and I knew that Jarvis wasn't really serious. It was just a metaphor, comparing his running skills to something that moved very fast.

Unfortunately for Jarvis, no matter how fast he was able to run, it wasn't going to be fast enough.

15

"I think I see where you dropped your phone," Jarvis said as he peered through the glass.

We were standing next to the closed garage door, staring out the window. The field of ivy was still alive, like a gigantic bowl of red and green spaghetti. Except the noodles were twisting and turning, burrowing back and forth and up and down over top one another.

And we were right in the middle of all of it.

"Can you see the phone?" I asked.

Jarvis shook his head. "No," he replied, "but I can

see the place where that vine grabbed you. Your phone can't be very far away."

"Are you sure we shouldn't just wait for Mr. Nelson to come back?" I asked.

"Face it, Kayla," Jarvis said. "As long as we're in this warehouse, we're sitting ducks. We're surrounded, and we can't go anywhere. There's no telling what those plants might do. They've already tried to kill both of us, and it's only a matter of time before the vines find their way into the warehouse. All I have to do is get your phone, and we can call for help."

"You make it sound easy," I said.

Jarvis heaved a nervous sigh. "Well," he said, "after all, they're only *plants*. They might be alive, but they can't have *brains*."

I thought about that for a moment. The idea of plants having brains seemed oddly strange, but then again, we didn't know what we were dealing with. I'd never heard of plants behaving like this before. I knew that some plants, like the Venus fly trap, are carnivorous in nature . . . but I didn't know of any plants anywhere in the world that attacked human beings or other animals.

The sun was still rising in the sky, and I figured that it was getting close to noon. There were some dark clouds way off to the west, and they looked like they might bring rain. But for now, the sky was blue, the sun was bright, and the air was warm and dry.

And the killer ivy was just as alive as ever.

"Okay," Jarvis said, taking a deep breath. "I'm ready. I'm going to run out there, find your phone, and run back. Close the door right behind me, but be ready to open it fast and let me in."

"Good luck," I said, knowing that it was meaningless, knowing that luck didn't have anything to do with it. Everything rested on how fast Jarvis could run, and if he could keep away from the vines of live, bloodthirsty ivy snaking across the field and the parking lot.

Jarvis threw open the door and bolted. I quickly pulled the door closed so hard that it caused the windows to rattle. Then, with my nose pressed against the window, I watched, my heart beating in time with Jarvis's racing footsteps.

I'm glad he's a fast runner, I thought, watching him run and leap and jump and dart around and over large clumps of moving vines. Some of the plants leapt at him, striking out like cobras, and several times Jarvis had to dash to the left or to the right to escape. The vines lashed at his pant legs, but he was moving so fast that none of them could get hold of him.

Without warning, he vanished. I couldn't tell if he fell, if a vine of ivy had grabbed him, or what. One minute he was running, and the next minute, he was gone. Had he fallen? Was he all right?

I needn't have worried. In the next instant, he popped up again. Only now, he had reversed direction, and he was running back toward the warehouse. His legs were churning and his arms were swinging wildly at his side as he raced through the parking lot that was becoming more and more filled with the tangles of ivy.

I began feeling more hopeful than ever. Jarvis was running incredibly fast, and he was easily able to escape the clutches of the slower-moving vines. In five seconds, he would be at the door, and I would open it and allow him through before closing it to keep the vicious plants from getting in.

But it wasn't the vines that caused a problem: it was simply human error. Jarvis was running incredibly fast. He made a leap over several vines and landed on his left foot, but his right foot smacked into the back of his left leg. He was down in an instant, face first, tumbling onto the ground.

And the vines were upon him.

"*Jarvis!*" I screamed, and my voice echoed through the empty warehouse. There was no one there to hear it except me.

I knew I had to do something.

But what? I didn't have any weapons to use to defend myself.

Frantically, I looked around the warehouse for something to use to help Jarvis.

The tractor, I thought. *Maybe I can use the tractor to save him!*

I shot a quick glance out the window, hoping to see Jarvis on his feet and running toward me.

Nope. He was on the ground, struggling to get up, while vines wormed over his body. I would have to hurry. He was thrashing and struggling, but now that he was on the ground, I knew that he wasn't going to have a fighting chance.

I raced to the tractor and climbed up into the seat.

My heart sank and my shoulders sagged when I saw the empty ignition.

No key.

Without a key, I wouldn't be able to get the tractor started.

Seated on the tractor, I again looked around the warehouse, and it didn't take me long to find something I had forgotten about:

The sickle!

It had been hanging on the wall all along, but because it was on the other side of the tractor, it was hidden from view!

I slid off the other side of the tractor and plopped to the ground. Grasping the sickle by the handle, I pulled it from the wall and made yet another discovery: there was a key dangling on the nail that held the sickle! The tool had been covering it up. It was a clever place to hide it, and I was sure it was the key to the tractor.

I paused for a moment, trying to decide what would be better: the tractor or the sickle. I quickly decided that the sickle would be of better use, as I would need it to hack at the vines that were attacking Jarvis.

Carrying the sickle like a spear, I raced around the back of the tractor and to the garage door, bursting outside and into the bright daylight. Only then could I hear Jarvis's voice

"Let go of me, you ugly, red worm!" he shouted. "Let me go! Let me go!"

"Jarvis!" I shrieked. *"Hang on! I'm coming!"*

Ignoring the mass of tangled ivy that licked at my feet and legs, I bounded across the parking lot, over the vines of red and green ivy leaves. When I reached Jarvis, I quickly assessed which vines were attacking him. Swinging the sickle with all my might, I began hacking away at the plants, viciously bringing down the metal blade and severing the vines.

"Don't hit me with that thing!" Jarvis screeched, when one of my swings came close to him.

"I won't!" I shouted. "I'm just trying to help you get free!"

As I chopped at more and more of the vines, Jarvis was able to pull the attacking plants away while using his pocket knife to saw through a vine. Finally, he pulled off the last one and scrambled to his feet. He folded the blade and returned the knife to his pocket.

"Come on!" I shouted, and we turned and began running back to the warehouse. Vines of red and green ivy continued to come at us, and I was amazed at how fast they were moving. In my mind, I had already compared them to snakes, but I couldn't help thinking about that again.

That's what they are, I thought. *These things are snakes. They're behaving just like snakes.*

Thankfully, we were able to make it back to the warehouse where we plunged through the open door. Jarvis slammed it shut behind him as I fell to the ground, still carrying the sickle with my right hand. Both of us were gasping, our lungs on fire from the burst of speed.

"All that," Jarvis said, between heaving breaths. "All that, and I didn't even get your phone."

"That's okay," I said. "At least you're alive."

I stood and looked out the window. Jarvis turned, and the two of us gazed out over the field of tangled, moving vines.

"Now what?" Jarvis asked.

"Now," I said defiantly, "now we get *serious.*"

Jarvis turned and looked at me. His face was a puzzle. "What do you mean?" he asked.

Using the sickle, I motioned to the tractor.

"Now, we're getting out of here."

Again, Jarvis looked at me with a puzzled expression on his face.

"What do you mean?" he asked.

"Just what I said," I replied. "We're getting out of here." I handed him the sickle, then walked to the tractor and around to the other side of it. I bent over and plucked the key off the nail in the wall. "Look what I found."

"The key to the tractor!" Jarvis exclaimed.

"Get ready," I said to Jarvis. "We're gettin' outta here."

He was still standing by the garage door. "You . . . you know how to drive that thing?" he asked in disbelief.

"My dad showed me how," I replied confidently. "We have a tractor just like it. It's a piece of cake."

Jarvis looked out the window. "But what are we going to *do* with it?" he asked.

"We'll drive this thing right through all of those vines," I replied. "Right up the driveway and out to the front gate."

I inserted the key into the ignition and turned it. The engine caught, and the tractor fired up. It coughed and sputtered to life, and the air was quickly filled with the choking stink of exhaust.

"I'm going to turn it around!" I said loudly. "When I get in front of the garage door, press the automatic button so it will open! Then, get on the tractor as fast as you can, and we'll get out of here!"

I put the tractor into reverse and backed it up a few feet. Then, I put it into forward gear, cranked the wheel, and turned it around. In seconds, the tractor was facing the large garage door, ready and waiting like an iron-muscled racehorse at the starting gate.

I nodded to Jarvis. "Okay," I said. "Press the button. Then, get on the tractor as fast as you can. When the door rises, we're taking off. And don't drop the sickle."

Jarvis pressed the button. There was a loud *thunk* and several clanking noises as the garage door in front of me began to rise, pulled by a rusty chain above us.

"Okay!" I shouted. *"Hurry! Get up here!"*

"I hope this thing moves fast!" Jarvis said, and he hustled over to the tractor and climbed up.

Although the seat was made for only one person, we were both able to fit on it. I gripped the big steering wheel, and Jarvis grabbed hold of the seat with his free hand. In his other, he carried the sickle.

As the garage door rolled up higher and higher, vines of red and green ivy began creeping into the warehouse. They were acting and behaving just like snakes, swerving and weaving back and forth.

"Hang on tight!" I ordered as I put the tractor into gear. I stomped on the accelerator, and the tractor jerked forward and nearly stalled; then, it bucked one more time and started moving. The front wheel rolled over some vines, and I gave it more gas.

"Don't stop!" Jarvis shouted over the roaring tractor engine.

"I won't!" I replied. *"Just hang on!"*

In seconds, we cleared the garage door and emerged from the shadow of the warehouse. The sun warmed my bare skin and stung my eyes.

I pressed on the accelerator, and the tractor sped

up. Although I should've been driving on the driveway, it was now so choked with vines of red and green ivy that it was nearly impossible to see the ground. It was also impossible to see where the driveway and parking lot ended and the field began. The vines were quickly taking over the entire farm.

"This is insane!" Jarvis shouted.

I didn't respond. Jarvis was right, of course, but at the moment, it didn't matter how crazy things were. What mattered most was getting away from the vines, getting away from the farm. I was sure that if we made it to the gate and onto the main road, we'd be safe. All we needed to do was make it through the tangled jungle of ivy that seemed to be getting thicker and thicker with each passing second.

Looking ahead, I tried to steer toward the easiest places for the tractor to travel, places that were less thick with ivy. No matter which way we went, we were going to have to go through the mass of tangled plants, as they had completely taken over the parking lot and the driveway.

But in the distance, I could see the front gate. Mr. Nelson had left it open, thankfully, and I knew that if we could make it that far, we'd be able to get away.

And we weren't going to stop, either. I was going to drive the tractor all the way home on the shoulder of the road, and I wasn't going to stop until we were safely parked in our driveway.

"Doesn't this thing go any faster?" Jarvis asked loudly.

I shook my head. "We're going about as fast as we can," I said as I carefully navigated the tractor through the vines. "My dad told me that tractors aren't made for speed; they're made for power."

"I guess that's a good thing," Jarvis said.

Still, I was having more and more difficulty. The vines were getting thicker and thicker, and they kept reaching up at us, licking at our legs, trying to grab us. Several of the vines wrapped themselves around the tires and the axle, and the engine bogged down a little bit. Once, my dad got our tractor stuck in the mud, and he had a difficult time getting it out. That's what this felt like. The farther we went, more vines came up at us. I know it sounds crazy, but it was as if they were all banding together in one effort, trying to stop the tractor.

Suddenly, the tractor slowed dramatically and came to an abrupt stop. I pressed the accelerator as far as it could go, but that only stalled the engine, and it died. I turned the key, and the engine roared to life again.

But the tractor wouldn't budge. I tried to back it up and then go forward, tried to rock it back and forth like I had seen my dad do, but it wouldn't work.

"Keep going!" Jarvis shouted

"I'm trying!" I yelled. *"But those vines have us all tied up!"*

Suddenly, I could feel the tractor moving, but it wasn't because I was doing anything. The front of the tractor was actually being raised into the air, like a bucking horse.

"Hang on!" I shouted. *"Hang—"*

In the next instant, Jarvis and I were thrown backward, tumbling off the tractor and into the tangle of angry, hungry vines!

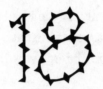

A few years ago, in our kitchen, I was leaning back in one of our dining room chairs. I was balancing myself on the rear two legs of the chair, using my fingers on the table to stabilize myself.

"Please don't do that," Mom warned. "You're going to fall."

"No, I won't," I replied, confident that nothing would go wrong.

As soon as I spoke those words, I lost my balance and began to fall backward. I flailed my arms in an attempt to shift myself forward and tried to grab the edge of the table, but it was too late. I crashed to the dining room floor, flat on my back.

Mom rushed to me and knelt. As soon as she found out that I was okay, she was mad.

"That's why you don't do that," she scolded. "Now, don't do that again. You were lucky, this time. Do it again, and you might not be so fortunate."

I felt a little silly. While I had been balancing on the two chair legs, I was certain that I wasn't going to fall. However, two seconds later, I was flat on my back on the floor.

But I'll never forget the feeling of being off-balance, in that brief moment when I lost control until I fell backward and hit the floor. I felt so helpless. Although I flailed my arms to try to regain my balance, to grab something that might stop my fall, it didn't help.

That's exactly what it felt like when I fell backward from the tractor. I flailed my arms madly, but there was nothing to grab onto, no way I'd be able to regain my balance. I tumbled backward off the tractor seat, flailing my arms and legs. And then, I was on the ground . . . sort of.

"Oof!" Jarvis gasped. He had landed first, and I had crashed down on top of him. He'd lost his wind when he hit the ground, but then I landed on top of him, giving him a double-whammy, really knocking the air from his lungs. I immediately felt bad for him, and I hoped he was okay, but now we had other things to worry about.

I rolled to my knees and jumped up. All around us, the ivy was moving, slithering about like live strands of thick, red and green spaghetti. And what was worse: some of the vines had grabbed the tractor. As incredible as it seemed, as unbelievable as it was, the ivy was pushing the tractor into the air!

Jarvis, still on his back, was gripping the sickle with his right hand. I grabbed the tool away from him.

"Jarvis!" I shrieked. "Jarvis! Get up! Get up! We've got to get out of here!"

Jarvis was clutching his gut with both hands now, trying to breathe. With my free hand, I reached down to help him, yanking him up from the ground.

"Can't . . . can't . . . breathe," he wheezed.

"We have to get back to the warehouse!" I shouted.

Already, some of the vines were trying to get at us. They were slithering around our feet and legs, curling around our ankles. I was easily able to kick them away, but I knew it wouldn't be long before they overtook us.

Frantically, I looked around, my head snapping back and forth. The gate was too far away, and there were too many vines in our path. And the warehouse, the building we'd just left, was quickly becoming overrun with vines. And the main office was too far away. There were just too many plants, and we'd never make it there.

We were left with only one choice: the irrigation barn. Already, vines were slithering toward it, but it was the closest building, and I thought we might have a chance to make it there. We would have to run over and through the jungle of vines, but it was our only chance.

"Follow me!" I ordered Jarvis. He was still having a hard time breathing, clutching his chest, but he managed to move. He stayed right behind me as I jogged over ivy. Vines came at us, and I used the sickle to hack at them, to cut them into pieces as we continued to move forward. We ran as fast as we could, but several times, we had to come to a complete stop when I had to use the sickle to clear our path of snake-like vines.

Again, I was completely amazed at how fast the ivy was growing. But I was even more amazed and puzzled at how it had come to life.

But those were things I could think about later. Right now, I had to concentrate on getting to the irrigation barn. I had to think about getting to safety.

Suddenly, Jarvis shouted, and I turned to see him fall flat on his face. A vine of ivy as big around as a garden hose had looped around his leg, tripping him. I quickly used the sickle to hack at the plant until Jarvis was free. Then, he leapt up, and we continued our trek.

Finally, we made it to the irrigation barn. The main doors were closed, but the side door was unlocked. I grabbed the handle, turned it, and pushed open the door. Jarvis was right behind me, and when he burst inside, I quickly slammed the door and bolted it. Then, I dropped the sickle and fell to my knees. We remained there, two kids on the floor, gasping for breath.

By no means was our ordeal over, but we were safe . . . at least for the moment.

We stepped away from the door and stared out the windows. After a few moments, Jarvis caught his breath.

"Why . . . why . . . why is . . . is this happening?" Jarvis stammered.

Slowly, dream-like, I shook my head. "I don't know," I said quietly. "It just doesn't make sense."

"I mean . . . I know that Mr. Nelson said that his ivy grows fast," Jarvis continued, "but plants aren't supposed to grow like that? Are they?"

Again, I shook my head. "I don't think so," I replied,

and my gaze shifted across the field, toward the open gate. I was hoping to see Mr. Nelson's truck coming back, boring through the tangle of ivy that now covered the gravel driveway. He would know something was seriously wrong, and he'd know that we'd be in trouble. He would come and help us.

But instead, all I saw was a thick mass of red and green ivy moving about, crawling over one another, in and around, back and forth.

They're nothing but snakes with leaves, I thought. *They look like plants, but they act like snakes.*

"Now what do we do?" Jarvis asked.

I looked around the inside of the building. Jarvis and I glanced at the old, blue truck at the same time.

"Are you thinking what I'm thinking?" asked Jarvis.

"I think so," I said. I nodded, but then I shook my head. I knew exactly what Jarvis was thinking, but I knew it wasn't a good idea.

"You saw what those things did to the tractor," I said. "If that ivy can stop the tractor, I'm sure the plants will be able to stop the truck, too. We're better off staying here. Let's look around to make sure that there isn't any place for the ivy to get in. If we can keep the plants from coming inside, we'll be okay until Mr. Nelson comes back."

On the other side of the windows, we could see ivy slithering up the glass. Some of the vines had reached the

108

roof.

And we could hear the plants scraping against the outside of the irrigation barn, too.

"Not only are they alive," Jarvis said, "but it's as if they have brains. It's like they're thinking."

"I'm glad you're here," I said to Jarvis. "Because nobody is going to believe this. If this happened only to me, everyone would say that I was making it up."

Jarvis shook his head. "You're not making it up," he said. "I'm seeing the same thing you are. Let's just hope we get out of here alive, so we can tell someone about it."

I hated just standing there, waiting and hoping. However, it seemed like the best thing to do at the time. I knew that if we tried something risky again, it would only mean trouble. And I also knew that Mr. Nelson *had* to be back soon. After all: he was only going to the hardware store. I expected to see his truck returning at any moment.

"Look at that," Jarvis said, pointing toward the window. I turned to see a green vine sweeping back and forth across the glass. However, while we watched, the tip of the vine began acting strangely. It began curling around, wadding itself into a ball. While we watched, it got bigger and bigger, until it was nearly the size of a volleyball.

All too late, we realized what was about to happen.
"Jarvis! Get back!" I shouted.

But before we could do anything, the ball of ivy

drew back on its stalk. It paused for a moment, then slammed itself into the window like a giant, green fist, shattering the glass and sending sharp, shiny shards into the room.

Vines of red and green ivy began pouring through the broken window like an ocean of death, their horrifying fingers reaching for us, twisting and turning. Once again, we were trapped, ambushed by sinister vegetation that would stop at nothing to get us.

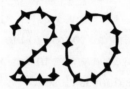

"To the truck!" I shouted, and I started running. Jarvis immediately followed.

"I thought you said the truck was a bad idea!" he shouted.

"Change of plans!" I replied. "We can't stay here! We have to try to make another run for it!"

I reached the truck, threw open the driver's side door, tossed in the sickle, and dove inside the cab. Jarvis followed, slamming the door closed. I climbed over to the passenger's side to give him some room.

Vines continued to pour in through the shattered window. They slithered down the wall and crawled onto the hard-packed ground.

"Do you know how to drive this thing?!?!" I asked.

Jarvis looked at the steering wheel and then at the dashboard.

"I think so," he said. "I mean, I've never driven a truck before. But I've seen my dad do it enough."

Thankfully, the key was in the ignition. Jarvis turned it, and the engine roared to life.

"But how are we going to get out of here?" Jarvis asked. "The garage door is closed."

"Smash through it!" I said. "This truck is big enough. The garage door won't stop it."

"We're going to get into a lot of trouble," Jarvis said as he reached up to the steering column and grasped the gear shift lever. As he dropped it into "drive," there was a loud clunking sound. The vehicle shivered.

"In case you haven't noticed," I said, "we're already in a lot of trouble! Right now, I care about being *alive!*"

I wriggled the sickle over my lap, as the garden tool barely fit into the cab. The long handle stretched across my lap and over Jarvis's legs, forming a seatbelt of sorts.

Jarvis turned the wheel and pressed on the accelerator. The truck jerked forward and turned to the left. He inched the vehicle forward even more, slowly turning

112

the truck so it wouldn't hit the wall in front of us.

"I hope I don't have to back this thing up!" Jarvis said. "I wouldn't know what to do!"

"You're doing fine," I said. "Just keep going. Turn it around and smash through the garage door."

"Are you sure you want to do this?" Jarvis asked as the truck continued to move.

"We don't have a choice," I said. "We have to get out of here. If this doesn't work, I don't know what's going to happen."

Already, the vines coming through the window had reached the floor. They were spreading out, reaching, turning, squirming and squiggling, coming toward the truck. It was as if they knew we were inside the cab.

Finally, we were facing the garage door.

"Okay," I told Jarvis. "Give it all you've got."

"I hope this works," Jarvis said. "I hope we make it through."

"Of course we will," I replied. "It's only a garage door. I've seen it on TV."

"Yeah," Jarvis said. "That's on TV. You can't believe *anything* you see on TV."

By now, the first few vines had reached the truck. They were ascending the front bumper, moving under the hood, and climbing next to me along the passenger door.

"Go!" I ordered.

Jarvis pressed the accelerator with his right foot, and the truck rocketed forward. I closed my eyes as we smashed into the garage door.

The crashing sounds were deafening. Glass shattered, wood splintered, metal screamed.

But the truck never stopped. Jarvis kept his foot on the accelerator, and the truck rocketed through without any trouble at all.

We were suddenly awash in sunlight. The truck bounced and rocked as it rolled over the crawling vines.

"The plants have completely covered the driveway!" Jarvis yelled.

"It doesn't matter!" I shouted. "Just keep going! Head for the gate, and don't stop!"

Quickly, however, we found out that the plan just wasn't going to work. The vines were too thick, and it wasn't long before the truck bogged down and began to slow.

"Keep going!" I shouted.

"I'm trying!" Jarvis shouted back. "But there are too many plants!"

The engine sputtered and coughed while Jarvis struggled to keep the truck moving forward. Unfortunately, nothing helped. The truck suddenly came to a halt, and the only thing we could see around us were red and green leafy vines. They whirled and swirled around the vehicle, blotting out the blue sky and the sun.

"Okay," I said, my voice filled with defeat. "Maybe this wasn't such a good idea, after all."

We were both breathing heavily, but neither of us spoke. I grasped the sickle on my lap.

"Do you think they can break through the glass?" Jarvis asked.

"I don't know," I replied. "I hope not."

I sighed, not knowing exactly what to do or what might happen next. In my mind, I hoped for the best, but I also expected the worst . . . which is exactly what happened.

I don't think I'd ever felt so helpless in my life. Sitting there in the truck with Jarvis, protected only by steel, metal, and glass, we could do nothing as the horrible plants swirled and swarmed around the outside of the vehicle. We could feel the truck being lifted off the ground, lurching back and forth, side to side. There were loud noises, bangs, and clanks, and I could hear pieces of the vehicle snapping. I only hoped that the glass would hold out, that the ivy wouldn't be able to get to us.

And the sickle in my hand wasn't too much comfort.

In fact, in the cab of the truck, it was worthless, because the garden tool was too big. I couldn't swing it or use the blade to defend us.

"Do you think it's possible Mr. Nelson isn't going to come back?" Jarvis asked.

"He has to," I replied. "He said he was going to the hardware store. He wanted to get there when it opened, so he could hurry back here."

"It sure is taking him a long time," Jarvis replied.

Beyond the glass, on the outside of the truck, the vines of red and green ivy swirled and squirmed. Blades of sunlight peeked through every now and then, but the plants were so thick that most of the sun's warm rays were blocked by the vines and leaves.

"I'm sorry I got you into this," I said. "This is all my fault. If I hadn't asked you to come help me, none of this would've happened."

"It's not your fault," Jarvis said, shaking his head. "You never could've known that this was going to happen. I'm sure Mr. Nelson had no idea that the plants would do this, either. Otherwise, he'd never have let two kids work here at his farm."

And for the time being, we were safe. Inside the cab of the truck, we were protected by the strong metal frame and shell.

But what if it doesn't hold out? I wondered. *What if*

it's not strong enough? What if Jarvis and I wind up getting crushed inside?

It was a horrible thought, and I knew that I had to push it away and replace it with a more positive outcome. Otherwise, I'd go crazy just thinking about it . . . especially with the live vines wrapping around us, tightening us in their green and red leafy fist.

The sound of the plants wrapping themselves around the vehicle, the scratching of the vines on windows and metal was driving me crazy. I turned on the radio, just to hear some background noise. A banjo twanged with plucking guitars. Jarvis didn't say a word. He just sat in the driver's seat, his hands on the steering wheel, the handle of the sickle resting on his lap.

A cloud fell over the sun, and the interior of the truck darkened even more.

And we could *feel* it. The shade provided by the cloud brought with it a strange sensation, and both Jarvis and I could sense something bizarre was about to happen.

And we were right.

The upbeat, happy country-western tune playing on the radio did nothing to lift my spirits. In fact, it made our situation seem even more gloomy than it already was, so I shut off the radio.

We waited.

After a moment, Jarvis spoke.

"Hey," he said. "Do you notice anything?"

I cocked my head to the side. "Like what?" I replied.

"Listen," Jarvis said.

I listened.

"I don't hear a thing," I replied.

"That's what I mean," Jarvis said. "And look." He raised his right hand and pointed at the windshield, at the leafy ivy covering the glass.

Suddenly, I realized what Jarvis had already noticed.

"The ivy!" I said. "It's stopped moving!"

All of the vines and leaves seemed frozen in place. They were no longer swirling and squiggling, and the only movement seemed to be caused by a gentle breeze that tickled some of the green and red leaves.

The sun, I thought. *There's a cloud over the sun. Could it be that the ivy doesn't move unless the sun is shining?*

We had our answer in the next instant. The cloud drifted to the east, and the sun came back out. Within seconds, the ivy was moving again.

"Jarvis!" I exclaimed. "It's the sun! The sun is making the ivy come alive!"

We peered through the windshield and up at the sky. The cloud that had covered the sun was slowly moving away, leaving a blazing, yellow globe in a canvas of hazy blue.

"Look!" Jarvis said, pointing off into the distance. "There's a big cloud coming! If it covers the sun, it's going to be there for a few minutes. We might be able to get the truck moving and blast through all of the plants!"

"That's what I was thinking," I replied. "If that cloud stays in front of the sun long enough, it might give us time to get out of here."

We waited while the cloud crawled slowly across the sky. It was big and fat and puffy, and its belly was a steely gray color.

"It's taking forever," Jarvis said.

"A watched pot never boils," I replied.

Jarvis frowned and looked at me. "What's that supposed to mean?"

"Oh," I replied, "it's just a saying that my mom says all the time. She says that if you watch a pot on the stove and wait for it to boil, it never will."

Jarvis thought about this. "That doesn't make sense," he said. "If you wait long enough, it *has* to boil."

"That's what I thought," I said. "But I gave up on trying to figure out my parents a long time ago."

"Me, too," Jarvis said. "I've never been able to figure out my parents, either."

"The cloud is almost over the sun," I said. "Get ready to hit the gas."

Gripping the steering wheel firmly with both hands, Jarvis sat in the driver's seat, ready to move. He looked a little funny, being that he was much smaller than an adult and looked very out of place in the cab of the truck.

123

The cloud drifted across the sun.

The sky darkened.

The ivy stopped moving.

"Go!" I blurted.

Jarvis didn't say a word. He slammed the accelerator to the floor with his right foot.

The engine revved.

The tires spun.

The truck shook and shuttered.

But it didn't move.

Jarvis raised his foot off the accelerator and then pressed it down again. Again, the engine revved, but the truck just barely moved.

"Try backing up!" I urged. "Put it into reverse, and then put it back into drive! That's how my dad rocks the tractor back and forth when it gets stuck in the mud!"

Jarvis tried rocking the truck, but it was useless. For whatever reason, perhaps because the ivy had lifted the truck off the ground, it wouldn't move more than an inch or two.

Peering through the windshield, I looked up at the sky.

"That's a big cloud," I said. "It's going to cover the sun for a few minutes. Let's get out and try to run!"

"Have you lost your mind?!?!" Jarvis asked.

"Jarvis!" I said. "It's the only chance we've got! It's

the biggest cloud in the sky! If we hurry, we can make it out to the highway!"

Jarvis looked up at the cloud, then through the vines. Although we couldn't see the gate or the highway, I already knew what he was thinking.

"We'll never make it to the gate in time," he said.

"But we could make it back to Mr. Nelson's office!" I said. "Let's stop talking about it and do it! Time's wasting!"

Without another word, Jarvis grabbed the door handle. He tried to push the door open, but the vines made it difficult. I crawled across the seat and helped him push. Finally, we were able to open the door far enough so that we could get out.

Jarvis was first, and I could tell he was a little nervous. Neither one of us wanted to even touch the ivy, but we didn't have a choice.

"Hurry!" I said as I slipped out of the truck behind him. I grabbed the sickle, and we began pushing our way through the tangle of green and red ivy vines.

"This is like the Amazon jungle!" Jarvis said, flailing his arms in front of him, pushing the vines away, trying to make a path.

"Here," I said, handing the sickle to Jarvis. "Use this. It might be easier than pushing those things out of your way."

While Jarvis hacked at the thick stems and vines, I remained right behind him. Every few seconds, I looked over my shoulder at the cloud slowly crossing the sky, covering the sun. Walking was difficult, because I had to step over vines and plants and push them out of the way as Jarvis hacked a large path with the sickle in front of me.

Ahead of us, through the vines, Mr. Nelson's office came into view.

"We're almost there!" Jarvis said.

Again, I looked up at the cloud, trying to estimate how much time we had.

We can do this, I told myself. *We can make it. We can do this.*

And we did.

Although the front door of the main office was covered with ivy, none of it was moving. Once again, they had turned into harmless plants, thanks to the cloud covering the sun.

Without any effort at all, we pushed the plants and vines away from the door and slipped inside. I closed the door behind us and locked it. Jarvis leaned the sickle against the wall, and both of us fell to the floor, panting and out of breath.

"We . . . we made it!" Jarvis said. "I don't know if we're safe, but we're better off being here than in the cab of that truck!"

I was about to speak when I heard another sound.

Honk! Honk-honk!

My eyes widened.

Jarvis's jaw fell.

Both of us leapt to our feet and bolted to the window. Even through the thick vines covering the glass, we could see across the farm, down the driveway.

Mr. Nelson's truck was by the gate!

We heard another honk, and the truck barreled forward, crashing through the tangle of vegetation.

"Finally!" Jarvis said, thrusting his fists into the air. "We're safe! We're going to be rescued!"

If only things were that simple . . . .

We watched as Mr. Nelson's truck ambled toward us, bobbing gently back and forth through the dense foliage. Although we knew the vehicle was traveling on the driveway, there were so many vines and leaves that it looked like Mr. Nelson was driving straight through a field of vegetation. The plants had completely covered the driveway.

Unfortunately, *that* was the problem. There were just too many plants, and it wasn't long before his truck got bogged down and wouldn't move any farther.

"What's he doing?" Jarvis asked, when he saw the truck stop.

"I don't think he can go any farther," I replied. "His truck is stuck. There are too many plants."

While we watched, Mr. Nelson emerged from his truck. He had to push away vines and leaves to get the door open, but he slowly began walking toward us.

I looked up at the sky.

The big, puffy, white cloud still hung in front of the sun, but it was moving, slowly crawling across the blue canopy. I tried to estimate how long it would take before the sun would come back out.

I looked at Mr. Nelson.

I looked up at the sky.

"He's not going to make it," I whispered.

"What do you mean?" Jarvis asked.

I cleared my throat and spoke in a normal voice. "Just what I said," I said, pointing up at the cloud. "If the sun comes out before Mr. Nelson makes it to us, the ivy is going to come alive again. Mr. Nelson doesn't have anything to defend himself with."

Jarvis looked up at the cloud and then back to Mr. Nelson. Mr. Nelson was making progress, but it was still a struggle for him. He had to push and sweep vines out of his way and step over the plants crisscrossing the driveway.

Jarvis cupped his hands around his mouth.

"Mr. Nelson!" he yelled. "Mr. Nelson! Hurry! The sun is going to be back out soon!"

Mr. Nelson stopped walking, paused, and cupped one hand around his ear, listening.

Like Jarvis had done, I cupped my hands around my mouth. "Hurry up!" I shouted, repeating Jarvis's words. I pointed at the cloud. "The sun will be out, and the plants will come alive again!"

I'm not sure if he heard us, but he continued walking toward us.

I looked up at the cloud. Most of it had passed over the sun, and it wouldn't be long before the big ball of yellow appeared in the blue sky.

I crossed my fingers on both hands. I know that things like that don't do any good, but I had to do *something*.

The field began to lighten and brighten, and the dull, murky cast slowly lifted. I looked up just in time to see a slice of yellow peek from behind the cloud.

I looked down and gazed around the field. The vines around the office slowly began to move, as if waking from a long sleep.

"Mr. Nelson!" I shouted. *"Run! Run!"*

But it was too late. In seconds, the cloud had passed by and the sun had appeared, hot and blazing and yellow in the blue sky. The vines, awakened once again by the powerful rays, came alive. They were ravenous and hungry. One of them wrapped itself around Mr. Nelson's legs, and he went down, face-first in the mass of plants. In seconds, dozens were on top of him, squirming and seething, twisting and turning.

Our hearts sank. There was nothing we could do.

"Mr. Nelson's not going to make it," Jarvis said somberly. "We're on our own."

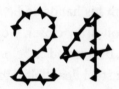

24

My knees went weak, and I felt dizzy. For a moment, I thought I was going to faint. I was so overwhelmed, so frightened, that my body and mind simply seemed to give up.

It took a moment, but I finally got hold of myself. Mr. Nelson was gone, and there was nothing I could do about it. I felt sad, because I really liked him. And I felt sad that he would be missed by his family and friends.

But I couldn't think about that at the moment. At the moment, Jarvis and I were still alive. Maybe if we were smart, if our luck changed, perhaps *we* could still survive.

"Look!" Jarvis suddenly shouted. *"Mr. Nelson isn't dead! He's up! He's up and running!"*

In the driveway, amidst the madness of swarming, snake-like plants, Mr. Nelson had somehow freed himself and gotten out. He was running like an Olympic sprinter, leaping over vines and bounding toward us. Plants lunged out at him like vipers, trying to seize him as he ran, but he slapped at them with his hands and continued running.

As Mr. Nelson drew closer, I opened the door. He burst through, and I slammed it behind him, turning the lock and sliding the steel deadbolt into place.

Mr. Nelson collapsed onto his knees, gasping for breath.

"You made it!" I exclaimed. "You're alive!"

Mr. Nelson nodded, closed his eyes, and took several deep breaths.

"What's happening?" Jarvis asked. "Why are these plants doing this?"

Mr. Nelson got to his feet. He was still out of breath, but he did his best to speak.

"I have no idea," he replied. "How long has this been going on?"

"Not very long," I replied. "Probably about an hour."

"We were hauling stuff to the dumpster when we noticed some of them moving," Jarvis said. "When they started attacking us, that was when we knew we were in trouble."

"We've been trying to get away from the farm ever since," I said. "But the plants won't let us."

"We noticed that when the sun is out, the ivy moves around and comes alive," Jarvis explained. "But when a cloud goes over the sun, they stop moving."

Mr. Nelson looked puzzled, and his face became a roadmap of confusion. "I don't understand why the plants have become so hyperactive," he said. "It's almost as if they've been given too much fertilizer."

"I was very careful to make sure I only poured in five gallons," Jarvis said, "just like you asked."

Mr. Nelson and I stared at him.

"What?" Jarvis asked. "What's the matter?"

"Jarvis!" I said. "You put five gallons of fertilizer in the irrigation tank?"

Jarvis nodded his head. "Mr. Nelson asked me to."

"I put in five gallons, too!" I said. "Didn't you hear Mr. Nelson when he told you *not* to put the five gallons in the tank?"

Now, it was Jarvis's turn to look puzzled. "No," he said, shaking his head. Then, he looked at Mr. Nelson. "I heard you yell to me, asking me to put the fertilizer in. Then, you said something else, but I didn't understand what it was."

135

"That was my fault," Mr. Nelson said. "Originally, I had asked you to put the fertilizer in. Then, I changed my mind. I thought you heard me tell you *not* to put the fertilizer in the tank."

Again, Jarvis shook his head. "Nope," he replied.

"So," I said, "that's why all of this is happening? Because the plants are over fertilized?"

"Most likely," Mr. Nelson said. "I can't think of any other reason. But don't worry. We're safe now. All we have to do is wait for the fertilizer to wear off, and that shouldn't take too long. In the meantime, we can stay here, in my office. The plants can't get to us while we're here."

An explosion of glass rang in my ears as the big window facing the field shattered. The building shook. Millions of tiny shards of glass rained down upon the floor, and vines of ivy began pouring in through the window, slithering down the wall and across the floor, moving toward us like deadly green and red snakes.

"Jarvis! Kayla! Follow me!"

Mr. Nelson bolted across the office and down a hallway and opened a door into a narrow stairwell. We followed him up to a landing where the stairs turned back and continued to go up. This led to a room with a low ceiling and what appeared to be a small trapdoor.

"This leads to the attic," Mr. Nelson said. "And another door opens to the roof." He pulled down the door, and a wooden ladder unfolded. Placing the legs on the floor, he looked at Jarvis and me.

"You guys go first," he said, gesturing with his hand.

This is insane, I thought. *This is totally insane. This is something that happens in movies and television, not in real life. Things like this are supposed to happen to someone else. Not me. Not me and my friends.*

I was first up the ladder. The attic was dark, and the only light came through the doorway in the attic floor. I cautiously moved back to make room for Jarvis, who was right behind me. Mr. Nelson followed.

"This way," he said, walking past me. "Be careful. There are no lights in the attic. But the door to the roof is over here."

The attic was dark and gloomy, but I didn't have any trouble following the big shadow of Mr. Nelson looming in front of me. He stopped briefly, and then light flooded in as he opened a door. A rectangle of light blossomed, and I followed Mr. Nelson through it, emerging into daylight onto a flat roof. Jarvis followed behind me, and the three of us stood, gazing out over the farm below.

"Spectacular," Mr. Nelson said.

"Well," I said, "I wouldn't necessarily call it *spectacular*."

"What I mean is," Mr. Nelson continued "that this is *incredible*. The ivy has grown so fast that it's completely overtaken the farm in just several hours."

It was true. From where we stood on the roof of Mr.

Nelson's office building, we could see all four corners of the farm. The entire driveway and the parking lot were covered with ivy, and in some places, it was five and six feet deep. We could see it climbing the old silo not far away, worming its way up over the irrigation tank, the barn, and the warehouse.

"Are you sure we're safe up here?" I asked.

"I think so," said Mr. Nelson. He walked toward the edge of the roof, but Jarvis and I stayed where we were. "In fact, there's an easy way to stop the plants. All we have to do is—"

Without any warning, a vine of red ivy appeared over the edge of the roof. It looped around Mr. Nelson's left ankle.

Then, in a split second, Mr. Nelson was gone. He didn't scream; he didn't shout. One moment he was standing there, in mid-sentence, and the next he was gone, pulled off the roof by the attacking ivy.

I shrieked, and Jarvis gasped. Both of us rushed to the edge of the roof and cautiously peered over the edge, watching for vines, wary that we might be the next two victims. Thankfully, there weren't any more plants close to the edge, and we were able to look down into the red and green leafy foliage.

Mr. Nelson was gone, and this time it was for real. Earlier, he'd been lucky enough to survive when he'd fallen in the driveway. He'd been able to get up and run, escaping the attacking ivy as he raced toward his office.

Now, his luck had changed. In fact, it had run out. *Completely.*

Mr. Nelson had just become the day's first victim.

"They got Mr. Nelson!" Jarvis shrieked.

I refused to believe it. My eyes searched the thick ivy below, looking for anything—a flash of clothing, a movement—any sign of life. I saw nothing. Mr. Nelson was gone, devoured by his own incredible ivy.

Finally, more vines began working their way up toward the roof, toward us, and it wasn't safe to remain near the edge anymore. We backed up closer to the attic door.

"We're trapped, Kayla," Jarvis said. "We can't go

downstairs, because the ivy broke the window, and the plants are probably already coming up through the building, looking for us."

"Don't be silly," I said. "Plants don't have eyes. They can't be looking for us."

"Well," Jarvis said defiantly, "the plants *know* where we are. Maybe they can *smell* us, or maybe they can just *sense* us. They *know* where we are, and they're coming for us."

As much as I hated to admit it, Jarvis was right. We were surrounded, and there was nowhere we could go. We were like two cornered cats, our backs against the wall, with nowhere to go, nowhere to run.

But . . . .

I looked up into the sky. To the west, a large, puffy, gray and white cloud was lumbering slowly toward the sun like a giant iron ship.

Mr. Nelson's last words echoed in my head.

There's an easy way to stop the plants, he'd said. *All we have to do is—*

What?

All we have to do is—

Then, it came to me in a sudden flash, like a lightning bolt searing through my brain.

"Jarvis! That's it!"

Jarvis frowned at me, puzzled. "What's it?" he

142

asked.

"I know what Mr. Nelson was talking about when he said that there was an easy way to stop the plants!"

27

"I don't know why I didn't think of it before!" I continued.

"Think of *what* before?" Jarvis asked. His voice was tense, insistent.

"The weed killer!" I said, throwing my hands, palms up, in front of me. "The weed killer that we saw in the warehouse yesterday! I'm sure that's what Mr. Nelson meant!"

Jarvis looked puzzled. "But how—"

"The 5,000 gallon irrigation tank!" I said, anticipating his question before he could ask. "If we pour the weed killer in the irrigation tank, it'll filter through the water and the sprinkler system! The weed killer will kill the ivy!"

Jarvis was still puzzled. "Are you sure it'll work?" he asked. "I mean . . . wouldn't it be easier to wait for the effects of the fertilizer to wear off?"

I shook my head. "We have no idea if the fertilizer will ever wear off," I said. "Maybe by using too much fertilizer, the change in the plants is permanent. Maybe they'll be this way forever. We've got to use the weed killer. We've got to destroy them!"

"But how?" Jarvis asked, and now it was his turn to place his hands out, palms up. Then, he swept his right arm in front of him, from left to right, motioning toward the ocean of swarming plants in the farm below. "I mean, look at this, Kayla. We're surrounded by ivy. The plants are alive, and they want us dead. How are we going to get to the irrigation barn without being killed?"

I pointed up at the giant, gray cloud. "That's it," I said to Jarvis. "That's our only hope, right there."

Jarvis tilted his head back and looked up.

"The cloud?" he asked.

I nodded. "That's a *big* cloud," I said. "It's going to cover the sun. And when it does, the plants will stop moving. That's going to be our only chance to get off this roof and to the irrigation barn."

The cloud inched along.

"How long do you think we'll have once the cloud goes over the sun?" Jarvis asked.

"I'm not sure," I replied, glancing up at the cloud and trying to estimate how long it would cover the sun. "I'd say about three minutes. Maybe four, if we're *really* lucky."

"Do you think we can make it all the way out to the barn before the sun comes back out again?" Jarvis asked.

"We'd better," I replied. "It's our only chance."

Slowly, a portion of the cloud drifted over the sun. All around us, throughout the field, the vines stopped moving. Slowly, all of the green and red plants froze in place. Everything became very still and quiet.

"Let's go for it!" I said, and I bolted through the attic door. Jarvis followed, and our footsteps pounded through the attic. We scrambled down the ladder like two crazed squirrels.

Four minutes, tops, I thought. *We've got to make it. We've got to make it to the irrigation barn and pour the weed killer in the irrigation tank.*

Then, I was struck with a funny thought. For some reason, I thought that if we didn't make it to the barn, I would never get my bicycle. That was the reason I had taken a job with Mr. Nelson at *Incredible Ivy* in the first place: I wanted a new bicycle.

Now, the only thing I wanted was to escape with my

life. I didn't care about a bicycle; I didn't care about anything else. The only thing I wanted was to be somewhere—anywhere—safe.

But first we were going to have to make it through a tangle of angry ivy . . . and that was going to be far more difficult than Jarvis and I could possibly have imagined.

We raced down the stairs and into Mr. Nelson's front office, which no longer looked like a place to conduct business; it looked like the Amazon rainforest. Vines of red and green ivy filled the room, looping and twisting around one another. Many of them reached as high as the ceiling.

And while I didn't want to touch any of them, I knew we were going to have to if we wanted to get out.

"There's the sickle!" Jarvis said, pointing to the floor. Bravely, he pushed aside thick vines and wide leaves, hustled to where the sickle lay, and picked it up. "We'll need this, for sure!"

"Let's hurry!" I said. "We don't have a lot of time!"

We were able to make it out of the office without using the sickle, because the plants weren't moving. Outside, I was relieved to find that the ivy wasn't as thick and tangled as it had been in the office.

I glanced up at the fat cloud. Nearly a minute had gone by, and I knew it wouldn't be long before the sun reappeared.

But we still had our work cut out for us. The foliage was so thick that we couldn't run, and Jarvis had to use the sickle, swinging it in front of him, hacking at the thick stems with the sharp blade. I remained behind him, a few steps away, giving him room to work.

High in the sky, the cloud continued its slow trek to the east.

I wanted to tell Jarvis to work faster, to swing harder, but I knew that he was doing the best he could. Besides: he wanted to get to the barn just as bad as me. If there was something we could have done to help us move faster, we both would've done it.

In my mind, I went over the things we would need to do. First, we would have to get to the barn, of course. Then, we would have to retrieve the big container of weed killer and pour it into the irrigation tank.

And we'd have to do it before the sun came back

out.

We forged ahead through the mass of tangled ivy. I didn't even like touching the stuff, knowing that it was far deadlier than any normal plant. I kept thinking that at any moment, one of the vines would reach out and wrap itself around my leg or arm or neck, but none did.

Finally, after what seemed like hours (it was really only about two minutes), we reached the barn. Pulling the ivy away from the door, Jarvis and I rushed inside.

"Over there!" I shouted. "It's that red container over there! The one with the black letters!"

We raced through the barn until we reached the large, barrel-shaped container. I grabbed one of the handles . . . and my heart sank. The container easily came up from the ground—much easier than it should have. If it was full, it would've taken both Jarvis and me to lift it.

"It's empty!" I cried. "I don't think there's a drop in it!"

Behind us, we heard a noise. Several of the vines in the open doorway began crawling to life. In the field, the red and green vegetation shined in the sun. The cloud had moved on.

"We're trapped," Jarvis said, his voice heavy with sorrow. "There's nowhere we can go. We're trapped here in the barn."

I shook my head. "It's not a barn anymore, Jarvis,"

151

I said.

"What do you mean?" asked Jarvis. "What are you talking about?"

"Exactly what I said," I replied. "The barn is about to become our coffin."

I was really, really scared.

Of course, being scared wasn't anything new. Lots of horrifying things had happened just within the last hour or so.

But now, Jarvis and I had come to the realization that there was no escape. There was absolutely no way we could get out. Mr. Nelson was gone, and we hadn't been able to call for help. We were trapped, surrounded by a field of thousands of deadly plants. Like I'd told Jarvis: the barn was about to become our coffin.

"Well, I'm not going to give up," Jarvis said. "I'm going to fight." He looked at me. "And you are, too. We're going to fight together, and we're going to get out of here."

I'll never forget how brave he looked at that very moment. Here we were, facing incredible odds, and Jarvis was standing tall. He wasn't going to admit defeat. Not yet, anyway.

That gave me hope. His determination and willpower gave me strength. Maybe the odds weren't in our favor, but Jarvis wasn't going to give up without a fight.

And neither was I.

"I need something to defend myself," I said, looking around the barn. Spotting two large doors, I ran to them. I figured it was some sort of storage area, and I hoped that perhaps I might be able to find something. A knife, a weed wacker, anything.

I pulled open the door and couldn't believe what I was staring at.

Tools, tools, and more tools. They were hanging on the walls, leaning against one another. The small room was filled with them.

But that's not all I was looking at. I was also looking at two large red containers with black letters that read: *WEED KILLER.*

Jarvis saw them, too, and rushed to my side.

"Kayla, you're a genius!" he said excitedly.

I shook my head. "No, I'm not," I replied. "All I did was open the doors."

I rushed forward and grasped the side of one of the containers. I tried to lift it. No way. It was just too heavy.

"And it's full!" I said as I grasped the other one and tried to lift. "This one is, too!"

"One problem," Jarvis said, turning around. He made a sweeping motion with the sickle in his hand. "Those vines aren't going to let up. How are we going to pour the weed killer into the irrigation tank?"

"I don't know," I replied. "But it's our only chance. If we don't get the weed killer into the irrigation tank, if it doesn't filter through the sprinkler system, then nothing is going to stop them. Not only will they get us, but just think of what happens if they overrun the farm. What will happen to the people at other farms not far away? What will happen to their livestock?"

"Are you saying that we have to pour the weed killer into the irrigation tank even while the ivy is trying to attack us?" Jarvis asked. His eyes were wide, and his mouth remained open.

I nodded slowly. "Yep," I said softly. "It's our only chance. Are you going to help me?"

"Well, I'm not going to let you do it alone," Jarvis replied.

"Okay," I said. "Here's what we'll do."

Quickly, I explained my idea to Jarvis. Even as I spoke, I doubted myself. I knew that what we were about to try wasn't going to work. I knew that, most likely, we were facing sudden death at the stem-like fingers of those vicious ivy plants.

But we had to try. However crazy it sounded, we were going to have to go out of the barn and face the tangled mass of angry, deadly vines . . . all by ourselves.

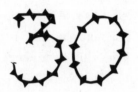

"Help me with this thing," I ordered, and I grabbed a handle on one of the containers. Jarvis shifted the sickle to his left hand. With his free hand, he grabbed the other handle.

"Okay, lift!" I said.

It took a lot of strength, but we were able to lift the container off the ground.

"Wait!" Jarvis said. "How are we going to pour it into the irrigation tank? This thing doesn't have a nozzle. If we try to pour it in, we'll spill it all over the place."

I looked around.

"There!" I said, and I lowered the container to the ground and rushed to the wall. Hanging on the nail was a yellow funnel, and I quickly snapped it up.

"This will work!" I replied. "This funnel will fit into the tank!"

I grasped the container again, and lifted. "Are you ready for this?" I asked Jarvis.

Jarvis nodded. "As ready as you are," he replied.

"Well, I'm not ready at all," I said, "but we don't have a choice. Let's get this done. Let's get this done, kill these plants, and get out of here!"

Already, the vines had found their way into the irrigation barn. Those crazy things were sweeping back and forth like so many snakes, their heads moving to the left and to the right. Actually, they didn't have heads or anything that even looked like reptiles, but that's the way they moved. Like snakes. Deadly, red and green snakes.

And we were going to walk right into the thick of them.

"Here's what we're going to do," I said. "The irrigation tank is only a few feet away, outside. As soon as we get to it, set the weed killer down. You get to work with that sickle, and keep the vines away from us. I'll unscrew the cap on the irrigation tank. When I get the funnel in place, drop the sickle and help me lift the container so we can pour the weed killer in."

"But if I drop the sickle, how am I going to keep the vines away?" Jarvis asked.

"We'll have to hurry," I replied. "Even if the vines wrap themselves around us, we have to keep pouring the weed killer in until it's empty."

"This is crazy," Jarvis said.

"It's *all* crazy," I replied. "Everything about this day is crazy. But just because we think it's crazy doesn't mean anything is going to change. Now, let's go."

Jarvis carried the sickle in his left hand and grasped the handle of the container with his right. I held the container with my left hand and the funnel in my right hand. Together, we hustled toward the barn door . . . and directly into the sea of angry, hungry ivy vines.

Walking into that wall of swarming vines was the scariest thing I'd ever done in my life. Mom and Dad always told me that sometimes you have to do things that you don't want to do. Sometimes you don't have any other choice.

They were right.

I mean, I guess that we actually *did* have another choice. We could stay in the barn, where we would face certain death from the attacking plants. That was our only other option.

And so, while I didn't want to put myself or Jarvis

in harm's way, it was the best choice we had. We would risk our lives for the small chance, however remote, of saving ourselves.

Walking into the jungle of vines was like walking into a mass of wild animals. They swarmed all around us, brushed up against our legs and arms, tried to wrap themselves around us.

While carrying the yellow funnel, I used my right hand to smack at the plants to try to keep them away. A vine wrapped around my neck, but I was able to pull it away before it tightened its grip.

We put the barrel down. The vines had grown up all around the irrigation tank, covering the cap. I pulled at some of the vines to get them out of the way, found the cap, and quickly unscrewed it. I dropped it, and it fell to the ground, but I didn't care.

Then, I unscrewed the lid on the container of weed killer. It, too, fell to the ground and vanished. I quickly shoved the yellow funnel into the irrigation tank's receptacle.

Meanwhile, using the sickle, Jarvis fended off the vines as best he could. I know it sounds crazy, but the plants seemed furious. They actually seemed mad at our presence, and they attacked us relentlessly.

Jarvis, however, worked hard with the sickle, chopping and hacking, keeping them away.

"The cap's off!" I shouted. "Help me lift the weed killer!"

Jarvis dropped the sickle. Both of us grabbed the handles at the top, bent down, and then used our free hands to grab the bottom of the container. We lifted it up, tilted it, and began pouring the weed killer into the funnel, which drained into the irrigation tank. Some of it spilled over the side, because we were pouring too fast.

"Hold it steady!" I shouted. "Try not to shake it around so much!"

"Those things are all over me!" Jarvis replied.

Not only were they all over Jarvis, the vines were attacking me, too. They wrapped themselves around my legs, my waist, everywhere. Still, I knew that we had to finish our job. After we emptied the weed killer into the irrigation tank, then, and only then, could we worry about the plants.

It took nearly a full minute to empty the weed killer into the irrigation tank, but it seemed like hours. Finally, when the container of weed killer was empty, we dropped it. By then, vines had wrapped themselves around the empty barrel and had begun to squeeze it. As soon as we let go of the empty container, the plants crushed it.

And Jarvis and I weren't fairing much better. We'd been seized by dozens of vines. They were all over us, and I used both hands to pull them away, to try to break them, to unwrap them from my legs and waist. A vine had wrapped itself around my chest and was squeezing so tightly that it was difficult to breathe, but I was able to yank it away.

Jarvis found the sickle he'd dropped and grabbed it. Then, we struggled and fought, pulling and hacking at the vines as we began to make our way back toward the barn. What would we do then? I didn't know. The vines had already found their way into the irrigation barn, so there was nowhere we could hide.

Unless—

The storage closet, I thought. *That might be a safe place. If we can get inside and close the doors, we'll have a chance.*

It was only a tiny spark of hope, but it was enough.

"Jarvis!" I shouted. "When we get to the barn, get inside the storage closet! If we can get in there and close the doors, we might have a chance!"

"But what about the weed killer?!?!" Jarvis shouted. "When is it going to kill the plants?!?!"

"It's going to take some time to filter through the water system and the sprinklers!" I said.

"How long?!?!"

"I have no idea!" I replied. "Just keep going!"

Jarvis continued hacking at the vines with the sickle. We made it through the barn doors, but by then, many vines had already made their way inside, slithering up the walls and around wooden posts.

But on the other side of the barn, the doors to the storage room were open, and no vines had overtaken that area.

Yet.

Shaking the last of the vines from us, we sprinted through the barn, nearly diving through the open doors of the storage unit. Jarvis dropped the sickle and crashed into the wall. I turned and grabbed one door, then the other. I slammed them shut, and darkness swallowed us.

"See if you can find a light," I said, panting. I was out of breath, and my heart was thrashing. I could hear Jarvis moving around in the darkness.

"Nothing!" he replied. Then: *"Wait!"*

There was a metallic clicking sound, the familiar sound of tiny metal beads against porcelain. A single light bloomed, and Jarvis suddenly appeared before me, holding a string in one hand. The string dangled from a single bulb above.

The light brought relief. Not much, but a little. At least we weren't in complete darkness, and I felt a little better about that.

"We've got to do something to keep these doors closed," I said to Jarvis. "They don't lock from the inside, so we've got to do something to keep the vines from—"

165

One of the doors suddenly exploded from its hinges. It was pulled backward into the barn where it was seized by dozens of long, green and red tentacles. The other door was next. It, too, was pulled away, crushed and broken by the vines.

Jarvis and I flung ourselves backward, pinning our backs to the wall of the storage unit. We grabbed whatever tools were available, anything we could use to defend ourselves. In my left hand, I held a crowbar and in my right, a garden rake. Jarvis had a shovel.

But it didn't matter. The entire doorway of the storage unit was soon filled with dozens—hundreds—of swarming, seething vines. They all came at us like a red and green army. We had no time to swing our tools, no time to use our weapons or defend ourselves. In moments, Jarvis and I were seized by the horrible tentacles, seized by dozens of wiry fingers that wrapped themselves around us tighter and tighter and tighter. A vine wrapped itself around my neck, but when I tried to reach up and pull it away, I found that other plants had already grabbed my arms. My legs, too. I couldn't move.

Worse: as the vine around my neck clenched tighter and tighter, I couldn't breathe. The vine tightened around my windpipe, cutting off my air. My vision clouded, and I began to see flashing stars. I was passing out.

This is it, I thought. *It's all over . . . .*

I tried to take a big gulp of air, but it was no use. The vine was too strong, too powerful, and had a choke hold around my neck. I couldn't even cough or gasp.

Suddenly, it loosened just a tiny bit. It was enough for me to take a gasp of air . . . and just in time, too. In another moment, I was sure I would have fainted.

The air filled my lungs and cleared my head. With renewed strength, I pulled at the vine still wrapped around my neck. I was surprised that I was actually able to get my fingers beneath it and pull it away. The vines around my arms, waist, and legs loosened their grips, too, and in a few seconds I was able to wriggle free.

Jarvis had succeeded in freeing himself, too. His shirt sleeve was torn near his left shoulder, but he wasn't injured. As for me, the only pain I felt was a stinging sensation around my neck where the vine had seized me. But it wasn't too bad, and the tight burning sensation was already fading away.

All around us, the vines moved to and fro, back and forth . . . but they weren't as frantic and fast as they had been. It was as if the plants were drifting off to sleep.

Jarvis and I watched the spectacle, amazed. Finally, all of the plants stopped moving. The two of us stood in the barn, surrounded by vines that crisscrossed the ground, creating a thick carpet of sorts. In some places, the vines were so thick that they were nearly up to our knees.

Jarvis spoke, and his words sounded distant, dream-like, as if he'd awakened from a deep, deep sleep. There was no excitement in his voice, no sense of victory or accomplishment.

"It worked," he said softly, gazing around. "The weed killer. It worked, just like we hoped it would."

Strangely, neither of us seemed very excited. I think we were simply too amazed that we had survived, amazed that we were even alive.

"It took a few minutes for the weed killer to work,"

I said. "It must've taken some time to soak into the ground and get to the roots. Once that happened, it must have killed the plants."

We continued standing in the barn, staring at the motionless red and green ivy strewn all over the place. Outside, a crow cawed several times.

We made it, I thought. *We're alive. We survived. We can go home.*

But Mr. Nelson hadn't been so fortunate. He'd been pulled from the roof of the office where he'd plummeted to his death, devoured by the very plants that he'd created, the ones he'd planted and raised.

But Mr. Nelson's death was *our* fault. Oh, we didn't do it on purpose. It was just an accident, a horrible, terrible mistake. He was gone, and we were responsible. If we hadn't accidentally filled the irrigation tank with twice the amount of plant fertilizer, none of this would've happened.

"Let's go," I said somberly. "We've got to get help. We've got to tell the police what happened."

Jarvis picked up the sickle that had been yanked out of his hands. He began hacking away at the dead vines, creating a path for us to walk. I cautiously pushed the plants away, wary that they might come alive at any moment.

Outside, the sun had fallen behind a cloud, and I was struck with a horrifying thought. I grabbed Jarvis's arm

169

and held tight.

"Wait a minute," I said. "Do you think the plants stopped because of the cloud? Maybe it wasn't the fertilizer that stopped them, after all."

Jarvis looked up at the giant, puffball-like cloud that blotted out the sun.

"I guess we'll know in a minute," he said. "If we hurry, though, we can get out of here before the sun comes back out."

He continued swinging the sickle, hacking and cutting at the red and green ivy. Here, out in the open, the plants were so thick that they rose above our heads. It was as if we were blazing a trail through a swampy jungle. A blanket of heat fell on my shoulders.

The sky lightened.

The red and green ivy brightened, shining in the sun.

In front of us, we could hear and see movement. Vines of ivy were twisting and turning, moving back and forth.

It had been the cloud, after all. It was the cloud that had stopped the plants, and not the weed killer.

Which meant that our nightmare wasn't over. Once again, we were in a lot of trouble. Here we were, standing in the middle of red and green ivy, surrounded by vicious, man-eating plants. This time, there was nowhere we could go. There was nowhere to run, nowhere to hide.

There was no way out.

This time, we were trapped for good.

"Hurry up!" I yelled.

"I'm hacking at these things as fast as I can!" Jarvis said. "There's no way we're going to make it through all of these plants and get out of the farm. We have to go back to the barn!"

"It's not going to be safe there, either!" I yelled. Panic and terror were rising inside of me like a black tide. My heart beat faster, and my blood pounded at my temples.

"Kayla? Jarvis? Is that you guys? Where are you? I can't see you."

It was Mr. Nelson!

Jarvis stopped swinging the sickle, and I stopped walking. The two of us froze. We were gasping for air, panting like exhausted dogs.

Then, I realized something. Not all of the plants were moving. The only ones that were moving were ahead of us, a short distance away. They weren't moving on their own . . . someone was moving the plants.

And that someone was Mr. Nelson!

Suddenly, he appeared in front of us. His hair was all messy, his shirt was ripped, and he was missing a shoe. But he was alive! He was okay!

"We thought you were dead!" Jarvis exclaimed.

Mr. Nelson nodded. "When that ivy yanked me off the roof," he said, "I thought I was dead, too. But the plants were so thick that they cushioned my fall. I was able to crawl away and hide in the crawl space beneath the office."

"We poured a bunch of weed killer into the irrigation tank," I explained. "I think it killed the ivy."

Mr. Nelson looked around. He reached out, grabbed one of the vines, and pulled it closer. He inspected it carefully.

"Excellent thinking!" he said. He was smiling.

"So, you're not mad?" I asked. Now that I knew he was alive, I thought he might be upset that we'd killed all of his plants. After all, he'd been working on this project for a long, long time. It was his dream.

"No, not at all," he replied. "I think we all learned a valuable lesson today. And besides: I don't think the plants are actually dead. I think the weed killer simply neutralized the fertilizer. I think when both of the agents wear off, the ivy will return to normal."

Well, maybe the plants were going to get back to normal, but I wasn't sure if I would. Jarvis and I had lived through the most horrifying experience of our lives, and I was sure I was going to have nightmares for weeks and weeks. Maybe even years.

Mr. Nelson offered to give us a ride home, but our bikes were still where we'd parked them earlier in the morning, so we hacked through the ivy to get to them and then rode home. On our way, we chattered like chipmunks, recalling and recounting the events of the morning. Sure, we'd been through a terrifying ordeal. But there was something about the entire experience that felt so exhilarating and exciting. While I would never want to go through something like that again, I felt proud that we'd lived through it. We hadn't been injured, despite the many dangerous and horrifying things that had happened.

"Do you realize how close we came to being plant food?" Jarvis said as we pedaled side by side along the shoulder of the road.

"We're lucky to be alive," I said.

"I wonder if your phone is still alive," Jarvis said.

I'd completely forgotten about my phone. Normally, if I would have lost or misplaced my phone, I would've been completely freaked out until I found it. Now, however, my phone didn't really matter all that much.

"I'll call Mr. Nelson tomorrow," I said. "He'll probably find it."

And that was pretty much the end of our horrifying adventure. Mr. Nelson had been correct: the effect of the weed killer had only neutralized the fertilizer. Yes, a good many of the plants died, but enough lived for Mr. Nelson to continue his farm and his experiments. I hope he succeeds.

Over the rest of the summer, I wound up taking babysitting jobs. I even mowed a few lawns. Finally, one week before school began, I'd earned enough money to buy my bicycle.

Jarvis was with me when I paid for it and rode it home. It was such a great feeling! Not only was it a super-cool bike, but I was proud of the fact that I had earned the money all by myself . . . something Jarvis had thought I'd never do.

"It sure looks cool," he said as we admired my bike in my front yard. We'd raced all the way to my house, and we had parked our bikes on the grass near the field where tall grass and brush grew. The day was a scorcher, the sun was high, and we were both sweating through our clothing.

We were standing near my new bike, admiring its red paint, shining in the sun like scarlet fire.

"I have an idea," Jarvis said. "Let's go for a trail ride."

"Okay," I replied, "but only for a short one. I have to go inside and get cleaned up for dinner soon."

There's a winding trail that begins in the field by our house. The grass and brush are overgrown, because nobody uses it very much. It has a lot of twists and turns and small hills, so on a bicycle, it's a lot of fun when you go fast.

I led the way, blazing down the trail as fast as I could, with branches and weeds licking at my legs. I could hear Jarvis laughing behind me as he tried to keep up.

Suddenly, I heard a crash and the sound of branches snapping. Jarvis abruptly stopped laughing, and I hit the brakes and halted my bike. I turned my head and looked back to see Jarvis's bicycle laying sideways on the trail. Nearby, branches were moving.

"Are you all right?" I shouted back to him.

Jarvis stood in waste-high weeds. He was smiling, and the sun reflected off his shiny helmet.

"No sweat," he said. "I just tried to take that turn a little too fast, that's all. I was—"

Without any warning, Jarvis was yanked to the ground. He let out a scream that was horrifying, a wail of pain and fear.

"Kayla!" he shrieked. "It's got me! The plant has got me!"

By then, I'd pushed the incident at *Incredible Ivy* to the back of my mind. Oh, I'd certainly thought about it now and then, sometimes more than others. But it was in the past, and I wanted to forget about it. It never occurred to me that perhaps some of Mr. Nelson's ivy had somehow been transplanted to another area . . . until I saw the green vine wrapped around Jarvis's leg.

I let my bike fall on the trail and raced to help my friend. Jarvis was rolling in the weeds, writhing and turning, still screaming in pain, pulling at the vine that had wrapped around his leg, just beneath his right knee.

"Jarvis!" I screamed. *"Hang on!"*

Jarvis suddenly rolled to his side, laughing.

"Hahaha!" he said, sitting upright and then standing up. "Gotcha!"

"But . . . but—" I stammered, bewildered.

"It's just some vine," Jarvis said with a wide grin. "I

fell by accident, but when I hit the ground, I saw this vine. It was just a joke. I wrapped it around my leg to fool you."

Then, he reached down and untangled the vine, letting it fall to the ground.

"It worked," I smirked. "You sure had me fooled."

Jarvis walked to his bike, grasped the handlebars, and stood it up.

"We'd better head back," I said. "If I'm late for dinner, my parents won't be happy."

I turned to get my bike and was surprised to find another kid on a bicycle coming toward me on the trail. He saw me just in time and swerved, but I still had to jump out of his way or else he would have hit me.

"Whoa!" I heard the kid shout as his bike skidded to a halt on the trail. He leapt off the seat and held his bike upright by the handlebars. "I'm so sorry about that!" he said. "I didn't mean to come so close to you, but I didn't see you from around the corner. Are you okay?"

"You missed me," I said, and to let him know that I wasn't mad, I smiled. He smiled back.

"Sorry," he repeated.

"Don't worry about it," he replied. "I'm Hunter Freebury. My family just moved to the big white farmhouse down the road." He hiked his thumb over his shoulder.

"The one with the horses?" Jarvis asked.

"Yep," Hunter replied, nodding. "We have two of

them. They belong to my two sisters. My dad promised them that when we moved to Iowa, they could have horses."

"And what did you get?" I asked. "A dog?"

Hunter shook his head. "I already have a cat," he replied. "His name is Bonkers, and he doesn't like dogs."

What kind of a name is Bonkers? I wondered, but I didn't say anything. Actually, the more I thought about it, the name *did* have a cute ring to it.

Bonkers.

"We moved here from North Carolina," Hunter continued. "My grandma owned the farmhouse, and when she died last year, my parents inherited it. So, we moved here."

I'd never been to North Carolina before, and I didn't know anyone who lived in the state.

"What's it like there?" I asked Hunter. "In North Carolina, I mean."

Hunter tilted his head and frowned. "Oh, it's pretty cool," he replied. "I have a lot of friends there. But in North Carolina, we lived in the city of Raleigh, and there aren't a lot of open fields like there are here in Iowa. And, of course, there was—"

He stopped speaking in the middle of his sentence, as if he'd forgotten what he was going to say.

"—there was *what?*" Jarvis asked, urging Hunter to

181

complete his sentence.

"Oh, nothing," Hunter replied. "You wouldn't believe me if I told you."

"Oh, you'd be surprised what we'd believe," I said, recalling our horrifying ordeal at Mr. Nelson's farm.

"No," Hunter said, shaking his head. "It's too crazy."

Now, I was really intrigued.

"Come on," I urged. "Tell us."

"Yeah," Jarvis said. "What's the big deal?"

"The big deal was in the ground," Hunter said.

I looked at Jarvis, and he looked at me. We exchanged puzzled glances.

"What was in the ground?" I asked. I was getting tired of prodding and poking around with questions, and I wished he would just tell us.

"Okay, I'll tell you," Hunter said. "But I have to go home for dinner first. Why don't you guys meet me in front of our house, and I'll tell you what happened. But I'm warning you now: what I tell you will probably give you nightmares. Don't blame me if you can't sleep."

Now, I was more interested than ever. And later that evening, after dinner, Jarvis and I met Hunter beneath a huge elm tree in his front yard. There, we sat in the grass and listened as he told us all about his harrowing experience with what he called the North Carolina Night Creatures . . . .

Next:

AMERICAN CHILLERS

AMERICA'S #1 SERIES FOR MAXIMUM CHILLS!

#41: North Carolina Night Creatures

Continue on for a FREE preview!

1

Whenever you wake up screaming in the middle of the night, you're bound to create a stir in your household. But when you wake up screaming *and* fall off the bed? Well, that's even *worse.*

And that's what happened to me one night in May. Or, *morning,* I should say, to make myself perfectly clear, because the clock on my night stand read 3:42 AM. So, to be completely truthful, I wasn't awakened in the middle of the night. It was very early in the morning.

But that really doesn't make any difference. All I remember was being chased by horrible creatures. In my nightmare, I was trying to run from them, trying to get away, but I couldn't move my legs fast enough. It was like I was trying to run in mud. The creatures were big, the size of humans, and they had claws like animals and wings like bats. They swarmed all around me, screeching and wailing. In my dream, I was screaming . . . but I didn't know that it was a dream. To me, it was so very, very real.

And *terrifying*.

But a sharp pain to my head knocked the dark fantasy out of my head, and I found myself in the darkness, the shred of a shrill scream on my tongue. My head was throbbing. I was sweating, and I was confused.

Where did they go? I wondered in a panic, snapping my head around, ready to dive for cover.

A distant patter of thumps quickly became a thunder of footsteps. A door burst open, and light flared. My eyes burned and I winced, covering my eyes with my forearm.

I was in my bedroom, of course. Dad and Mom stood in my bedroom doorway, looking worried and concerned. My oldest sister, Shaina, stood behind Mom, peering around her. Next to Shaina was Abby, who is one year older than me. Dad was in his blue pajamas; Shaina, Abby and Mom were in their nightgowns. For a brief instant, they all looked like pale ghosts.

"Hunter!" Mom exclaimed. *"Are you all right?!?!"*

I moved my arm and rubbed the sore spot on my head. I'd fallen out of bed, and most likely banged my head on the hard wood floor.

"I . . . I was having a nightmare," I stammered. "There were all sorts of weird creatures chasing after me, and I couldn't get away. I guess I fell out of bed."

"Smooth move, knucklehead," Shaina said, rolling her sleepy eyes.

"Hush, Shaina," Mom said, glancing down at my sister. Then, she stepped toward me and knelt down. She felt my head with the palm of her hand.

"Ouch," I said.

"You're going to have an egg there," Mom said, "but I think you'll be fine. Just a bump."

"You're lucky nothing fell out," Abby said.

"That's enough, girls," Dad grumbled. "Go back

to bed."

My sisters vanished.

"Well, now that we know the world's not ending, I'm going back to bed, too," Dad said, and he turned and walked away.

"Are you sure you're all right?" Mom asked me.

"Yeah," I said, and I climbed to my feet.

"I'll get you a glass of water," Mom said. "You get back in bed."

Mom left, and I climbed back into bed. The sheets and covers were a mess from my kicking and thrashing. After rearranging them and pulling them up to my neck, Mom returned, carrying a glass of water. She sat on my bed and handed me the glass. I sipped.

"What was your dream about?" she asked.

"Monsters," I replied. "They were chasing me, and I couldn't get away."

"That's because of all those scary books you read," Mom said.

I shook my head. "No, it's not," I replied.

But, then again, I couldn't be sure. I loved to read scary books, and maybe they were the reason I had so many nightmares. Some of the books I read were so terrifying that I had to sleep with the light on.

Still, I loved reading them, and I wasn't going to quit, even if they did give me scary dreams.

I drank half the glass of water, then placed it on my night stand.

"Well," Mom said as she stood. "Try to get back to sleep. And try not to have any more bad dreams."

"Okay," I said.

Mom shut off the light and closed the door, leaving it open just a crack. A thin sliver of amber glowed, coming from the nightlight in the hall. The light was welcome and comforting, and the darkness in my room didn't seem so scary. I closed my eyes . . . but only for a moment.

Suddenly, I heard a faint scratching on my window screen, and my eyes flew open. The window was closed, of course, because the night was chilly. But I could still hear the faint scratching against the screen, like the sound of a metal zipper slowing being pulled up and down, up and down . . . .

And why did I decide to get up to see what it was?

I don't know, especially after having such a horrifying nightmare. But I knew that if I called for Mom and Dad, they'd probably get mad when they discovered that it was only some insect or moth on the screen. No doubt Shaina and Abby would come running, too, and they would make fun of me for days, telling everyone that I got scared by a puny little bug.

So, very slowly, I climbed out of bed.

I crept to the window.

Slowly, using my index finger on my right hand, I pulled open the drape, staring in disbelief.

When I saw what was on the screen, I flinched. Then, I drew in a quick breath and held it, surprised and in disbelief over what I was seeing.

"Wow," I whispered.

It was only a beetle . . . but he was *huge*. He was as big as my thumb, and probably the biggest insect I'd ever seen in my life. Ever since I was a little kid, I have always been fascinated with bugs. I was always catching them in jars and trying to find out their proper names. In some cases, I memorized their

Latin names, speaking them out loud to myself for practice so I would be sure to say them right. At school, it was fun to tell my friends that I had caught a *Nematocera Culicidae*. Most of my friends would frown and wonder what in the world I was talking about when I use words like this. Of course, a *Nematocera Culicidae* is simply the Latin name for an ordinary mosquito, but my friends didn't know that.

But the beetle crawling around on my screen? I had no idea what it was. All I knew was that he was gigantic, and if it hadn't been the middle of the night, I would have rushed outside with my insect net and a jar to catch him. I would love to get a better look at him in the daylight.

However, it was dark. Even in the faint glow of the streetlights, I couldn't see too many of the insect's features, except the silhouette of his long, oblong body and his six legs, along with two fat antennas protruding from his head.

I watched him crawl on the screen for an inch or two, stop, then crawl some more, then stop again.

For whatever reason, I reached my hand up, extending my insect finger. Just as I was about to touch the screen where the insect was, he flew off with a furious clapping sound. His wings were loud, and the creature sounded like a tiny airplane taking flight. He was so big that I could see his figure in the glow of the street light, and I watched as the insect landed in the yard.

Too bad it's not daytime, I thought. If it was, I'd go out and catch that thing in a jar.

I climbed back in to bed and closed my eyes. Soon, I fell asleep.

In the morning, I'd forgotten all about the dream I'd had the night before. I forgot about the insect on the screen. The only thing I was aware of when I woke up was being hungry. So, I tumbled out of bed, found my slippers, and made my way to the kitchen.

The house was quiet, and I was the only one awake. Shaina and Abby always slept in. Usually, Mom more Dad had to wake them up to get them out of bed.

But not me. During the summer, I was always up early, usually right when the sun came up. Summer meant no school, and I was going to make the most of every day.

I poured a bowl of cereal and grabbed a half gallon milk from the fridge. Then, I sat at the kitchen table to eat and read the back of the cereal box. Cereal boxes always had something interesting to say, and, once in a while, there was a prize hidden inside. Mostly, it was just useless junk. But it was still fun to get something free.

Something I was reading triggered my memory, and I suddenly remembered the insect I'd discovered on the screen the night before. Once again, I wished that I'd discovered the creature during the daylight hours. I would have caught him, for sure.

After finishing my cereal, I rinsed the bowl and spoon and put them in the dishwasher. I returned the milk to the fridge.

What am I going to do today? I wondered. It had been sunny and hot for the past few days, but I'd heard that rain was supposed to move in today. That would most likely mean that I'd be inside, and not playing outdoors with my friends. I mean, if it only rained a little, that wouldn't be any big deal. But Mom and Dad didn't like me playing outside during thunderstorms. They were always afraid that I'd get hit by lightning.

I strode through the kitchen, into the living room, and to the big window that overlooks our front yard. Mom's blue van was parked in the driveway, and there were two cars parked in the driveway across the street. The sky was faint gray, covered by a layer of clouds. Although it wasn't raining yet, it looked like the weather forecasters were going to be right, after all.

I was about to head to my bedroom and change into my clothes, when something in the yard caught my attention.

Dirt.

In the middle of the front yard, there was a small pile of dirt, as if the lawn had been chewed up, or someone had dug a hole. I moved closer to the window and peered curiously at the strange sight, trying to remember what had happened the day before that might have caused the earth in the front yard to be disturbed. Mom or Dad wouldn't have done anything like that, I'm sure. Dad freaks out if you mess with his lawn. He keeps it mowed and watered so it always looks perfect. If my sisters or I would have dug a hole or somehow damaged the lawn, Dad would have grounded us until we graduated from high school. Which, for me, was a long way off, because I'm only eleven.

At the time, I'd completely forgotten about the

195

giant beetle that I'd found buzzing at my screen the night before. I'd forgotten that the insect had flown off and landed somewhere in the yard.

Those were things that I would remember later, when I started to figure things out, when I began to put two and two together. That was when an ordinary, average day in Raleigh, North Carolina would take some very strange—and horrifying—turns.

Still puzzled about the mound of dirt in the yard, I pulled myself away from the window and padded back to my bedroom. I flipped on the light and changed into a pair of jeans and a T-shirt, found my tennis shoes, and slipped them on.

I turned off the light. Just as I was leaving my room, a scratching sound caught my attention. I stopped and turned, gazing around my murky room.

I clicked the light on.

Scratch. Scra-Scratch.

It was coming from my window. Something was scratching at the screen.

I walked to it, reached out, and drew the curtain back with my hand, expecting to see the beetle or some other sort of insect.

There was nothing there.

I held the drape open and gazed into the yard. Once again, my eyes caught the small mound of dirt in the middle of the lawn.

After standing at my window for a few moments and not hearing the sound again, I let go of the curtain and allowed it to close. Then, I turned and walked out of my bedroom, clicking off the light as I left.

I walked by Shaina's bedroom. Even though her door was closed, I could hear her snoring. She snores just about every night, and she sounds like a semi-truck. She snores louder than my dad.

In the living room closet, I found my sweatshirt and pulled it on over my head. Quietly, I slipped out the front door.

The morning air was cool, but it wouldn't be long before summer's heat awoke from its slumber. Summer days can be unbearably hot in North Carolina, even on cloudy days like this one.

I leapt off the porch and jogged across the lawn, stopping as I reached the pile of dirt. I kneeled.

The dirt was clumped in a small, beach ball-sized area. And it appeared freshly-moved, too. I grabbed a clump of it and let the gritty, cool sand fall through my fingers. Then I turned and looked at my window.

Somewhere, a bird called. I could also make out the sounds of cars on the distant freeway, a familiar, droning hum that I heard often. For some reason, it sounded strange.

I looked around the neighborhood.

There was no one else in sight, no one was moving. Even grouchy old Mr. Millard, our next door neighbor, hadn't been out to get his newspaper. It was still rolled up and laying on the first step of his porch.

I looked at my window again. Beneath it, and growing all along the front of the house to the porch, was a band of thick, leafy, spinach-colored shrubbery.

Something had been scratching on my window. Last night, it had been a beetle.

But he'd flown away, I thought. *He'd flown away and landed—*

I looked at the small pile of disturbed earth by

my feet.

—here. He landed in the grass, right here.

Now, something else had been scratching at the screen.

I walked toward my bedroom window and stopped at the edge of the shrubbery. I peered at the screen and all around the pane, looking for signs of the insect. I thought that perhaps he'd returned, and maybe he'd made the same scratching sounds just moments before, when I'd been in my room.

No beetle.

I was disappointed, because I thought I might have another chance to catch him. It would be cool to put him in a jar and keep him for a while. He would have been easy to catch, and I'm certain he wasn't dangerous. I didn't think he'd bite me, or anything. Plus, both of my sisters hated bugs and spiders. It would have been fun to freak them out!

I turned and stared back at the mound of disturbed earth, the clump of dirt on the cool, dew-covered grass.

Was it possible that the beetle somehow did that? I wondered. He was big, for sure . . . but it didn't seem possible that it would have been able to create such a large disturbance in the lawn.

Suddenly, I felt a sharp, painful stinging sensation on my ankle, just above my tennis shoe . . . and that's the moment that I realized that maybe the beetle was dangerous, after all . . . .

4

I yelped and leapt away from the bushes, reaching down to swat the giant beetle, or whatever it was, off my leg.

There was nothing there.

I looked all over my shoe, my sock, and my pant leg, but I didn't find an insect.

Moving closer to the bushes, I searched the leafy vegetation. I didn't find an insect, but suddenly, near my feet, a small branch moved.

I took a step back and knelt down. As I did, the

shrubbery suddenly exploded, and an enormous, human sized insect attacked!

Except it wasn't an insect at all. It was Lindsay Morford! She had been hiding in the bushes all along, waiting for me!

When she leapt out, she roared like a lion and raised her arms like a bear. Yes, she surprised me, but I can't say that I was *scared.* She looked too funny, and there were curled green leaves and jagged twigs on her baseball cap and stuck to her gray sweatshirt.

"Hahahaha!" she said, lowering her hands and placing them on her hips. "Now, *that* was funny!"

I smiled and nodded. "You got me, all right," I said. "I thought you were a giant beetle."

Lindsay looked down at herself, then looked at me and rolled her eyes. "I think I can see the resemblance," she said, brushing herself off and adjusting her ball cap. "But I don't feel like a bug."

"How long were you there?" I asked, pointing to the bushes.

Lindsay shrugged. "Oh, ten minutes, I guess. I tried scraping on the screen with my fingernails to scare you awake, but it didn't work."

I shook my head. "I heard you," I replied. "I was

already up. I thought that the sound might be coming from a huge beetle that was at my screen last night."

Lindsay's eyes lit up. "I saw one of those, too," she said. "In fact, I caught it and I put it in a shoe box."

"You did?" I asked. "Where is it now?"

"In our garage," Lindsay replied, hiking her thumb over her shoulder. "I left it there last night. I guess I forgot about him until just now. Want to see him?"

"Are you kidding?!?!" I asked. "I wanted so bad to catch him last night, but he flew away. Besides: I don't think my parents would have been real happy about me chasing around a bug in the yard in the middle of the night."

"Come on," Lindsay said. "I'll show you the one I caught."

We walked, side by side, to Lindsay's house, completely unaware of the horrifying surprise we were about to find waiting for us in a dark corner of Lindsay's garage.

ABOUT THE AUTHOR

Johnathan Rand has been called 'one of the most prolific authors of the century.' He has authored more than 75 books since the year 2000, with well over 4 million copies in print. His series include the incredibly popular **AMERICAN CHILLERS, MICHIGAN CHILLERS, FREDDIE FERNORTNER, FEARLESS FIRST GRADER,** and **THE ADVENTURE CLUB.** He's also co-authored a novel for teens (with Christopher Knight) entitled **PANDEMIA.** When not traveling, Rand lives in northern Michigan with his wife and three dogs. He is also the only author in the world to have a store that sells only his works: **CHILLERMANIA!** is located in Indian River, Michigan and is open year round. Johnathan Rand is not always at the store, but he has been known to drop by frequently. Find out more at:

www.americanchillers.com

ATTENTION YOUNG AUTHORS!
DON'T MISS

JOHNATHAN RAND'S

AUTHOR QUEST

THE DEFINITIVE WRITER'S CAMP
FOR SERIOUS YOUNG WRITERS

If you want to sharpen your writing skills, become a better writer, and have a blast, Johnathan Rand's Author Quest is for you!

Designed exclusively for young writers, Author Quest is 4 days/3 nights of writing courses, instruction, and classes in the secluded wilds of northern lower Michigan. Oh, there are lots of other fun indoor and outdoor activities, too . . . but the main focus of Author Quest is about becoming an even better writer! Instructors include published authors and (of course!) Johnathan Rand. No matter what kind of writing you enjoy: fiction, non-fiction, fantasy, thriller/horror, humor, mystery, history . . . this camp is designed for writers who have this in common: they LOVE to write, and they want to improve their skills!

For complete details and an application, visit:

www.americanchillers.com

Johnathan Rand travels internationally
for school visits and book signings! For
booking information, call:

1 (231) 238-0338!

All AudioCraft books are proudly printed, bound, and manufactured in the United States of America, utilizing American resources, labor, and materials.

USA